# Mist Rider

Dawn came up that day in the town of Random on a bad note. They found a respected local man dead, hanged by the neck from the tree in the livery corral. And things were about to get worse with the discovery of the victims of murderous slaughter and rape at a nearby homestead.

Were the two events linked? Was a bunch of crazed killers on the rampage; a lone gunman hell-bent on some personal retribution? The days that followed drifted from fear into nightmare as the town and its folk fell prey to the torment of Edrow Scoone and his ruthless sidekicks.

But then a stranger, scarred and silent, booked himself a room at the Golden Gaze saloon. . . .

# Mist Rider

LUTHER CHANCE

A Black Horse Western

ROBERT HALE · LONDON

ISBN 978-0-7090-8473-0

Robert Hale Limited
Clerkenwell House
Clerkenwell Green
London EC1R 0HT

www.halebooks.com

Typeset by
Derek Doyle & Associates, Shaw Heath
Printed and bound in Great Britain by
Antony Rowe Limited, Wiltshire

*This one especially for Sharon*

# CHAPTER ONE

The swish of saloon bar-owner Lanky Joe's besom across the boardwalk fronting the Golden Gaze had signalled the start of the day in Random for more years than most folk could remember.

It was a morning ritual, a tradition that had etched itself deep into town lore. Few men stirred till Lanky had raised the first dust. He was never late, never early, and a whole sight more reliable than many of the timepieces gracing the fancy vests of some town men. Lanky and his besom were the very essence, it seemed, of time itself.

But today was different.

There had been the usual creak of the batwings, sure enough, the first sounds of Lanky's shuffled steps, the swish of the besom, and then, as if smothered, a total, almost suffocating silence.

The break with the familiar had not escaped Ben McKellan in the room above his main street store and general mercantile. He was one of the first to a window to see for himself why there had been only one swish and then nothing. But what he saw when he parted the drapes and blinked on the early dawn light, left him none the wiser.

Lanky was there on the boardwalk, besom in hand as ever, but today he was staring down the street beyond Cuts

Bailey's barbering shop, Charlie Mint's saddlery, towards Jed Chargers' livery, the forge, stablings and gated corral.

And he was staring with the look of a man who could neither take in nor believe what he was seeing.

It took the storekeeper just three minutes to finish dressing, settle his hat, unlock the store and step into the street, by which time he had been joined by Cuts Bailey and a still sleepy-eyed Charlie Mint.

'Just what's goin' on here?' mumbled Charlie, flicking his braces over his shoulders. 'What's with Lanky?'

'It's what he ain't doin' that's the puzzlement,' said Cuts as the three men crossed the street to the saloon.

'Mornin', Lanky,' greeted McKellan. 'T'ain't like you to hold up on the cleanin', 'specially at this hour. Damn it, we've gotten to rely on you for time-keepin'. What's the problem? You not feelin' well? You seen somethin' as don't. . . .'

The storekeeper's voice drifted to no more than a gasped breath as he followed Lanky's raised arm to where it pointed to the livery.

'Oh, my God,' murmured Charlie.

'What the. . . ? Who the. . . ?' stumbled Cuts before swallowing what seemed like a mouthful of sand.

'In the name of. . . .' began McKellan, but lost his voice again.

The four men stared through the soft morning glow at the body of a man hanging from a noosed rope slung and secured over the main branch of a tree in the corner of the corral.

'Is that who I think it is?' murmured Lanky, his eyes narrowing on the silhouetted shape of the body. 'Is that—'

'Jed Chargers,' said McKellan in little more than a whisper. 'We'd best go rouse the sheriff.'

# CHAPTER TWO

'Been dead some hours. Midnight or thereabouts.' Doc Marchman came slowly upright from his squatting position by the side of the body, closed his medicine bag with a decisive click and adjusted his hat thoughtfully. 'Now just who in tarnation would want to set about hangin' a man like Jed Chargers?'

The gathering of town men at Doc's back murmured and muttered among themselves until a lone voice broke above the drone.

'Tell you one thing, Doc, if that's the work of one of us – somebody we know to in this town – he's a dead man walkin'.'

'You can bet to that.'

'S'right. We'll find him.'

'And hang him just like he's done for Jed there!'

'Not before we've half strangled him!'

'Gutted him!'

'I'm for takin' the biggest, sharpest blade I can lay a hand to and—'

'Whoa, there. Steady up.' Sheriff Caulk stepped clear of the crowd of men, turned to face them and raised his arms for quiet. 'Know how you feel,' he began in a softer, easier tone. 'Cuttin' down Jed's body just now was the worst moment of my life and, like you, I want the scumbag who did it.'

The town men erupted in another surge of muttering.

'But we can't – and we won't – get to a lynchin' just to satisfy heated blood,' continued the sheriff, raising his voice. 'I ain't got a notion, not in my wildest thoughts, as to who might have done this or why. I'm goin' to need time to take a closer look, reckon things through, consider them – and that's what you're goin' to give me: time. So I want you all to get back to your homes, go about your business and leave me to do the job you good folk pay me for.

'That ain't to say, mark you, as how I don't need your help. I do. Anythin' you see, hear, think of that don't fit, I want to know of it, 'specially if it's connected with Jed, however remote. Understand? You hearin' me? Good. Then let's get to it, shall we?'

Doc Marchman waited until the town men were beginning to disperse before moving to the sheriff's side. He laid a hand on his shoulder. 'Well done. Could've been a tricky situation.'

'They're shocked, they're angry, and they ain't never seen nothin' like it in Random before – 'specially in Random. We just ain't that sort of town,' said Caulk.

He nodded as the men passed from the morbid scene at the corral and made their slow, silent way down the main street, some to their homes, some to gather in small groups, others in anticipation of an early opening at the Golden Gaze.

'They'll simmer down long enough for us to mebbe make some sense of this,' said Doc. 'But where to begin? That's the problem.'

'One thing's for sure, this ain't the doin' of one man. Single fella operatin' on his own would have to get a whole

10

heap lucky to pull this off without raisin' a sound. Somebody would've heard. No, this was the work of two, perhaps three men.' The sheriff raised his hat and ran his fingers through the wisps of thinning hair. 'But why?' he frowned. 'Where's the motive?'

'Anythin' taken?' asked Doc.

'Young Pete Phillips who helped Jed here says not – leastways not that he can see so far. Says he'll stay on to run this place, see to the stock for the time bein' 'til things are sorted, and keep checkin' meantime. But on the face of it' – Caulk shrugged his shoulders despairingly – 'there's nothin' to say who, why, precisely when or to what end. Damn it, Jed was as clean livin' along of the best. He wouldn't have crushed so much as a fly out of any malice. Just weren't in his nature.'

Doc collected his bag. 'I'll see as how the body's moved and we set a time for a decent burial. Least we can do. Jed have any kin?'

'Not known. No, there was just him, this place, the horses. Jed didn't care for much else.'

Doc grunted as he turned to the dusty street. 'Know what bothers me, Sheriff?'

'I got a mountain botherin' me,' said Caulk. 'You may as well add to it!'

'If it weren't town men who strung Jed up, then it must be strangers. Outsiders. Men we don't know and ain't never seen before. So where are they now?'

Much the same train of thought occupied the minds of those still gathered in the boardwalk shade.

The shock of the killing had given way to anger, a simmering fury that one of the town's own – a highly respected member of the community – had been so chillingly murdered for no good reason, leastways none anyone could point to. Why, was the first question. If nothing had been taken from the livery, there was no obvious answer. Which quickly led to asking: who, and the distinctly chilling prospects that quickly surfaced. . . .

'Strangers – it's gotta be strangers. Ain't no other explanation,' pronounced a man in a moth-eaten straw hat. 'Some parts of the territory's chokin' with 'em. I hear tell there's any number trekkin' west not twenty miles north of here. No sayin' to what strangers get up to, is there?'

Some men nodded and murmured in agreement, others were more sceptical.

'When strangers – drifters more like – get to doin' somethin', they're doin' it with a purpose in mind,' said a man with a large paunch and a whiskey-nurtured glow. 'What *purpose* was there here? None. Why come off the main trail just to hang a man at midnight?'

'Revenge,' said an older man, burying his nose in a crumpled rag. 'Retribution.' The man blew into the rag. 'Mebbe Jed had a past we didn't know to. Mebbe somebody finally caught up with him.'

'Don't sound much like Jed to me,' grimaced a doubtful onlooker. 'I've known Jed these past ten years. If Jed had a past I'd have known to it.'

'Folk don't always get to sayin',' said a shy man beaded with a glistening sweat. 'Pasts are kinda personal.'

The gathering fell to an uneasy silence as they listened to the swish and sweep of Lanky Joe's besom and watched the clouds of dust shimmer in the strengthening sunlight.

'Supposin' whoever killed Jed comes back,' said a tall, wrangling man, twisting a length of rope through his fingers.

'What's that supposed to mean?' asked the man in the straw hat.

'Why would they do that?' said the man with the rag.

'I'm just supposin', that's all. Nothin' we can think to so far makes any sense, so why not suppose them murderers have got another reason. They could come back. They might figure—'

The man with the paunch hitched his pants. 'If they did come back,' he began, his dark eyes narrowing. 'If they did have the Godalmighty, sonofabitch cheek to so much as show their faces—'

It was at this moment that Lanky Joe swished his besom through a decisive last attack on the morning's dust and announced that the saloon was opening early 'on account of the circumstances'.

Something to settle the nerves, agreed the town men making their way to the spotless boardwalk.

The sun was hot and high when young Pete Phillips, doing his best to keep the dozen horses stabled at the livery to their daily routine, took a break and strolled into the deeper shade of the long barn.

He narrowed his gaze on the shimmering open country to the north and pondered yet again just who had ridden in at midnight intent on killing Jed Chargers. He shook his head in answer to his own thoughts. There was no answer; nothing made sense; it was all a crazy jumble.

He tightened his gaze and concentrated.

Rider coming in; slow pace, no hurry. He knew that horse, sure he did. Patsy Newbutt's roan mare. Shod it here only last week. So why was Patsy riding in today? This was a busy time of the year for her pa and brother back at the family homestead. Maybe the mare needed looking to.

No, not the mare. In fact, not the horse at all. It was Patsy who needed tending – if there was still time.

# CHAPTER THREE

Sheriff Caulk stepped softly into Doc Marchman's back parlour where the drapes shaded out the fierce sunlight, removed his hat, coughed lightly and waited.

It was some minutes before Doc appeared from the spare bedroom, closing the door quietly behind him.

'How is she?' asked Caulk, turning his hat anxiously through his gnarled fingers.

Doc sighed, crossed to the table in the centre of the room and poured himself a glass of lemonade. 'Cool drink?' he offered. Caulk shook his head. Doc sank a long gulp of the liquid and blinked his eyes clear of concentration. 'She ain't good, and that's for sure,' he continued, wandering to the window overlooking the long stretches of barren land. 'Sleepin' right now, which is best for her. I've done all I can for the time bein'.'

Caulk swallowed. 'She say anythin' about what happened?'

'No,' said Doc carefully, 'but I can imagine.' He turned sharply. 'You got anybody out there?'

'Joe Dimes and Fisty Fox rode out fast a half-hour ago.' He hesitated a moment, the hat spinning through his fingers like a wheel. 'I'll be frank, Doc, I got dark thoughts about this. Nothin' makes sense – 'ceptin' what I ain't for acceptin'. Patsy's mare comin' in like that; and her in that condition—'

'Raped,' said Doc bluntly, his eyes suddenly bright and fierce. He placed a hand on the table. 'Patsy was raped out there. And God knows what else. Ain't no other way of puttin' it.'

Caulk's hat spun to a halt. His fingers relaxed. His face drained to a sickly grey. 'But. . . .'

Doc crossed to a cabinet, opened one of the double doors and produced a bottle of whiskey and glasses. 'I have a feelin' we're both headin' for the Newbutt place. We'll go together, just as soon as Ma Brown gets here to watch over Patsy. I've sent for her. Meantime, you look in need of a shot of this.' He poured a measure of the whiskey and handed it to Caulk. 'Me too,' he added, pouring a second measure.

The fly skimmed angrily over the surface of the hot sand, hovered as if calculating distance and headed for the congealed pool of blood on the floor of the homestead veranda.

Joe Dimes disregarded the intrusion and went back to fumbling to light a cheroot. His fingers shook, his head was spinning, his eyes blurred, and the icy chill in his gut seemed to deepen and turn colder. He wanted to vomit, but his nerves were too knotted. Maybe he would wake in a sweat to find this had all been a nightmare, that there had not been the blood-soaked bodies of Elmer Newbutt and his son John, no ransacked homestead, no shattered crockery, torn drapes and bedding, no smashed furniture, bloodstained walls and floors, and no staring eyes of the dead. . . .

The match flame flared, the cheroot glowed. Joe

walked into the deeper shade, disturbing the fly as he went.

'Who, damnit, who?' groaned Sheriff Caulk, his fingers drumming his frustration on the clapboard wall of the home as he joined Joe in the shade.

'A madman, for sure,' said Joe, drawing on the cheroot. He released the smoke. 'More like mad*men*. This is the work of more than one fella.'

Caulk turned from the wall, narrowed his eyes and stared into the sprawl of the empty land. 'They must've ridden in at sun-up,' he began reflectively. 'Three, mebbe four of 'em, I'd guess. Tracks show they came from the east. So what – perhaps who – is east of here?'

Joe blew a long stream of smoke. 'Not a deal,' he shrugged. 'Leastways, not to my knowledge. But if these scumbags are straight up drifters, they could've come from anywhere. Whole territory gets to be littered with 'em from time to time.'

Both men turned as Doc and Fisty emerged from the homestead living area and joined them.

'These rats ain't no ordinary drifters,' said Doc, drying his hands on an already stained cloth. 'They didn't take anythin'. Nothin' as I can see to.'

'When drifters hit a place like this, they're usually in need of more than a killin' and havin' themselves a woman,' added Fisty. He removed his hat and wiped the band with a bandanna. 'Food, water, money, horses . . . Somethin'. They always want somethin'. These fellas simply trashed the place, shot Elmer and John and raped Patsy.'

'Hell, she was lucky,' said Joe. 'Lucky to be alive when the scum rode on, and lucky that mare of hers had the instinct to head for town. It must've known. But what that gal must be thinkin' right now. . . .'

'One thing's for sure,' said the sheriff, his gaze tightening on the land, the rocks, rough brush and scrub to the far horizon, 'I'm goin' to personally put the rope round the necks of whoever did this.'

'Same as we're goin' to hang whoever did for poor old Jed,' echoed Fisty, settling his hat with a tight-lipped determination.

Doc laid aside the cloth. 'Might be one and the same person or persons,' he said quietly.

Sheriff Caulk, Joe Dimes and Fisty Fox stared at him in silence.

'You don't mean—' murmured Joe.

'The *same?*' frowned Fisty. 'But that . . . no, t'ain't possible, is it?'

'Don't see why not,' said Doc. 'Three killin's in the space of a few hours. Nothin' taken at either place. No motive, savin' somebody's desire to get their grubby hands on Patsy. And in both the killin's, whoever did it just rode out.'

'Doc's got a point here,' said Caulk. 'And figure this: we wouldn't have known what had happened out here if Patsy had not reached town in the state she did and in the way she did. Mebbe the rats who hit this spread intended she should stay alive. Mebbe they *helped* her into the saddle.' He held up a cautionary hand. 'But before you say it, don't ask me why, 'cus I ain't got a notion.'

'And don't ask me neither,' said Doc. 'If my reckonin' is right, there's only one thing we can do.'

'And what's that, Doc?' asked Joe, the cheroot hanging unsmoked in his fingers.

'We wait.'

'Wait?' grimaced Fisty.

'Just that,' said Doc. 'It could be that Patsy will recall somethin' of what one of the men here said. Mebbe she heard somethin', saw somethin'. What would be a waste of time right now is saddlin' up a posse to go ridin' hell-for-leather round the territory in search of fellas we don't know to and ain't never seen.' He paused thoughtfully. 'I've a feelin' these men are set on some crazy mission, and they ain't through with it yet. They'll be back.'

The fierce afternoon light had eased to the glow of the cooler evening by the time the four town men were satisfied they had done all they could at the homestead for the time being.

They buried the bodies of Elmer Newbutt and his son John in the shade of a lone tree at the far end of the corral. 'Only fittin' they should rest here,' Sheriff Caulk had said. 'Elmer and his wife built this place. He wouldn't want to be leavin' it now.'

Fisty Fox had volunteered to remain at the spread to 'look to the stock and tidy the home up some' until Patsy could make whatever arrangements she came to reckon best. ' 'Sides,' Fisty had added, 'you never know I might get to findin' somethin' that tells us who the varmints are. Or I might see—'

'Don't you go addin' to the body count, you hear?' Caulk had ordered. 'I'll have more men out here just as soon as I can get 'em organized and I've spoken to Patsy. Just stick to the stock-mindin', Fisty, and get some sleep – if you can in a place like this. . . .'

The sheriff was right, Fisty mused, some hours later when he stood alone on the homestead veranda, the spread already had its ghosts.

Was there a chilled edge to the night air, or was he

imagining it? Was there a whispering breeze through the dark scrub, or was it voices he could hear? Did the shadows move, or simply lengthen? And why did he feel he was being watched?

Well, maybe he was, he thought, as he focused yet again on the blurred shape far to the north. Was that a rider out there? Was he watching the homestead? Just how long had he been there? If it was a lone rider, then why the hell—?

And then he was gone. Just like that. Here one minute, nothing the next, and Fisty was alone again.

Or was he?

# CHAPTER FOUR

It rained that night; long, deep rain that settled like glass in the first downpour before seeping slowly through the baked Midwest dirt. Clouds rolled and rumbled through the intense black of night where lightning cleaved the darkness fast as a blade. A high wind raced through town, setting hanging lanterns swaying, doors, windows and loose boards creaking, and what dust remained clear of the rain to scurrying slivers that headed for cover in waiting cracks.

Lanky Joe's besom was at work at the first hint of the limp, wet dawn, but the swishes and sweeps had none of their usual vigour, and the dust heavy with the damp, no inclination to swirl. Not that Lanky's efforts were at their sharpest. He had too much to think about, too many possibilities to reckon, too many theories to figure and fathom.

Talk in the saloon until nearing midnight had been of nothing save the hanging of Jed Chargers and the massacre at the Newbutt spread. Wild speculation and almost instant rumours were rampant.

'I hear as how young Patsy saw the faces of them rats clear as day.'

'That ain't so. They say she won't never speak again. Too deep in shock.'

'There's a bunch of the scum rangin' the whole territory. Twenty or thirty strong.'

'They're led by a crazed half-breed.'

'They've killed close on a hundred.'

'They burn and rape and pillage as they go. Ain't nobody can stop 'em. . . .'

But the harsh facts were that nobody knew or had the remotest notion who had committed the atrocities. It was as if, as Ben McKellan put it, they had blown in on a bad wind, reaped their destruction, and moved on.

Or had they? This unknown had fired its own round of speculation.

'They'll stay just as long as the pickin's are easy and there ain't no law to halt 'em.'

'They'll ride ten, twenty miles out, then wait, then . . . back again. More killin', more blood.'

'Types like them keep comin' back. We'll be like a feedin' ground.'

'Ain't goin' to be nobody safe. Not a man, not a woman, not even a child.'

' 'Specially women. They sometimes take women. Yeah, that's right – force 'em to ride with 'em. Use 'em 'til they're dead, then feed 'em to dogs.'

'Somethin' like that happened down South. They took more than a dozen young gals. Weren't one of 'em lived.'

'They could take every woman in town. . . .'

Lanky's handful of bar girls had taken particular fright at this and disappeared behind closed – and sometimes locked – doors.

Some younger men had been only too anxious to boast their willingness to take on any danger single-handed.

'Give me a gun – a prized Winchester; give me a horse – one of them black mares poor Jed set such store by, and I'll ride. Sure, I will. Ride 'til I catch up with them sonsofbitches – and then watch me. Won't be one left standin!'

'Take out whoever's leadin' 'em, that's the secret. Pin him and you've got the whole stinkin' heap of 'em. That's how it's done.'

'Throw down the challenge. I'm for a showdown. A shoot-out. Takes guts to face up, one to one.'

'Don't see no point to waitin'. Don't go along with that. No point. I'm for gettin' to 'em, anytime you like. Sun-up won't be too soon.'

'Right now, if I had my way. . . .'

It had been left to old Pop Ryder to calm the young bloods with the canny observation that there was nobody to shoot at right now. 'Get to whippin' yourselves up like that and you'll be pluggin' your own feet!'

The appearance in the saloon of Sheriff Caulk accompanied by Joe Dimes put an end to the talk and banter. Caulk urged the town men to get back to their homes. 'Ain't no more to be done here, men. Tomorrow's another day and things might be lookin' a whole sight better.'

'Not for some,' quipped a younger man. 'The dead don't get to seein' things better.'

'We owe the dead our respect,' Caulk had retorted. 'But they sure as hell wouldn't want us to sit about threatenin' what we *might* do. Mebbe our time will come. God willin' it will and these scum will be brought to justice. But meantime, there's practical things need tendin'.'

'You name it,' said Pop. 'Ain't no shortage of fellas here.'

'I need three or four men to work a rota system of lookin' to the Newbutt spread. Fisty's out there right now, and Patsy ain't in no fit state to be makin' decisions about the place.'

'She said anythin' yet, Sheriff?' asked a man at the bar.

'Not yet, but we ain't for hurryin' her. Doc's sittin' along of her. Patsy will talk when she's ready.' He paused, his gaze taking in the faces turned to him. 'I'm mountin' a night patrol for a while. Nothin' permanent, but it might be wise for a few nights at least. Not that I figure for them killers returnin' – doubt if they'd have the nerve – but we'd best be on our guard. Anybody here willin' to help give your name to Joe. Now let's call it a day, eh, fellas? Time for some sleep. . . .'

It was soon after the men finally cleared the saloon that the first rains blew in from the north, filling the night and the darkness with a sorrow that seemed to Lanky to be eerily fitting.

The town of Random had passed into mourning.


Lanky swished the besom through the last of the damp dust and brought it to rest. He leaned thoughtfully on the handle for a moment, his gaze taking in the length of the empty street, the smudged morning light where the early grey threatened more rain to come.

His thoughts turned to wondering what sort of a nightmare the dark had been for Patsy Newbutt. Maybe Doc had ensured she slept. He hoped so. And how many ghosts had come to haunt the family spread? Had Fisty Fox seen any of them?

He sighed. Twenty years of building his life in Random, most of them spent in the effort of putting the Golden Gaze on a business footing that gave him a living; no wife, no kin, but he was his own man, respected, regarded around town and owing no one. Now, in what still seemed a dark dream, the town, his life, the future had been dragged into misery. Or would it pass? Would the days as they had always known them return? There would be scars for some, memories fired in hell for the likes of Patsy Newbutt, but. . . .

Lanky's eyes narrowed. The light was poor, but, damn it, he was as near certain as he would ever be that there was a rider out there, side of the tree where Jed had hanged. A lone rider, dark, almost a silhouette.

Just sitting, watching, maybe waiting.

# CHAPTER FIVE

Lanky had laid aside his besom, wiped his hands on his apron and taken three steps from the boardwalk to the street with the intention of reporting what he thought he had seen to Sheriff Caulk, when he was hailed from the general store by Ben McKellan.

'All quiet, Lanky?' called the storeman, closing the door to the store behind him. 'I'm a light sleeper, but the night seemed quiet enough to me.'

'You see anythin'?' asked Lanky as Ben approached.

'Nothin' save the sheriff's men on patrol. Why, did you?'

'I ain't sure,' said Lanky, blinking. He turned his gaze to the tree by the livery corral and scratched his head. 'Mebbe, mebbe not. Can't be sure. Thought I saw a man . . . a rider . . . dark-lookin' fella . . . dark horse . . . over there, at the corral. But I could be mistaken. Times like these do strange things to a fella's thinkin'.'

'You can say that again,' said Ben, adjusting the set of his jacket across his shoulders. 'I ain't been thinkin' straight since . . . since seein' Caulk cut down Jed's body. Then there's that poor gal, Patsy, her pa and brother gone, and her in the state she is. I tell you straight . . . Lanky, you listenin' to me here?'

'Sorry,' fumbled Lanky, pulling his gaze away from the corral. 'I was just thinkin', if I did see a fella out there, what was he doin' just sittin' there, watchin'? Where'd he come from? And why didn't he come closer?'

'How long was he there?'

'Can't say. I'd finished sweepin', just looked up and, hey presto, he was there, like magic. Then you called across and he was gone.'

'Young Pete's been at the livery all night, mebbe he saw somethin'.'

Lanky shrugged. 'Could be. It's just odd, that's all.'

'Ain't nothin' that ain't odd round here at the moment,' quipped Ben. He laid a hand on Lanky's shoulder. 'What say we go see if one of them pretty gals of yours has done the decent thing and brewed some fresh coffee?'

'Now that does make sense!' smiled Lanky.

The two men left the street to the slow grey light and the first spots of more rain.


The rain was steady, the light greyer when Doc Marchman hurried along the street to the sheriff's office.

'If ain't one thing it's another,' said Doc, swishing the rain from his hat as he opened the door and stepped inside. Rain'll mebbe cool it down some, in more senses than one,' he said, accepting a mug of coffee offered by Caulk.

'Any news?' asked the sheriff, struggling to hide the anxiety in his voice. His gaze settled tight on Doc's face. 'Patsy,' was all he added.

'She's awake and we've talked – but only briefly,' said Doc.

'And?'

Doc sipped quietly at his coffee. The rain rushed suddenly on a swirl of wind at the office window. Caulk

26

waited, his stare tightening.

'Four men approached the Newbutt spread that mornin',' began Doc.

'Four?' repeated Caulk, frowning. 'Hell . . . four. Did she recognize any of 'em? Did she—?'

'Ease up there. Can appreciate how you're feelin' and needin' to do somethin', 'specially to keep the townfolk calm, but you've gotta let me tell this as Patsy put it. Not that there's a deal as yet. It's all goin' to take time. Right now it's too close, too damn vivid for her. Understandable.'

'Sure. Sorry.'

There was another rush of wind and rain at the window. 'Like I said, four men rode in. Came down from the north and looked to Patsy like they'd been ridin' some days, mebbe weeks. Chances were they needed food and water for themselves and their horses. They looked real rough – men and horses. But that weren't nothin' new to the Newbutts. Drifters often passed through always in need of somethin' to eat, some place to wash up, mebbe to sleep for a couple of nights. Sometimes they offered to pay – but mostly not – or do a day's work. But Elmer was never fussed. Did what he could out of his natural generosity. He was like that.'

'Say that again,' said Caulk, watching the rain streak the window.

'These rats asked for nothin',' Doc continued flatly, a cold edge to his voice. 'Hardly said a word, accordin' to Patsy. Just sat there, starin', spittin', grinnin'. Then . . . Then one of 'em drew his gun and shot Elmer point blank. Another did the same to John, again point blank.' He hesitated. 'It was then they turned their attention to Patsy.'

'All four?'

'One after the other. Passed her round like a bottle.'

Caulk swallowed and moved closer to the window. 'Hell,' he murmured, his voice grating. 'How'd she manage to get clear? She say anythin' about that?'

Doc took a slow turn round the office and paused again at the sheriff's desk. 'That's the worryin' part,' he began. 'Seems like my figurin' might have been right.'

Caulk turned his gaze from the window. 'How come? You mean them fellas wanted Patsy to ride for town?'

'Seems like it. She remembers bein' dragged on to her horse. She recalls leavin' the spread and seein' the blur of the town and movin' steadily towards it. Then – nothin', not 'til she found herself in a bed at my place.'

'Hmm,' murmured Caulk. 'And what do we reckon from that?'

Doc shrugged. 'A threat? A warnin'? Somebody tryin' to say somethin' in a grim kinda way? But why? Say what? Whatever it is they're tryin' to get over ain't reached us yet, neither in the hangin' of Jed nor in the killin's at the spread. All they've done is spook a whole town into jumpin' at its own shadow.'

'Mebbe that's exactly what they wanted. Fear.'

A fresh gust of wind threw rain at the window.


Business at the Golden Gaze was brisk long before noon. Town men took shelter against the persistent rain – or claimed that was the reason for their being in the saloon at that hour – and were only too grateful for the company, to join in the talk of the killings, the abuse of Patsy Newbutt and speculate for the hundredth time on who might be responsible. There was safety in numbers, and few were anxious to leave.

'Don't much matter who did it,' said a man, seated with

three others at a corner table. 'Whoever they are, they ain't here now. And ain't likely to be. My guess is they're long gone, way over the border, or mebbe into them hills west of Two Forks. Fella could lose himself for a lifetime out there.'

'I don't buy that,' frowned Cuts Bailey from where he stood at the bar. 'I don't see how anybody can say them killers are gone. They ain't in town, that's for sure, but that ain't to say they've left the territory. They could be anywhere out there. Five, six, a dozen miles out of town in any direction you care to choose. Fact is, we don't know. We don't know who they are, where they hail from, why they did what they did, where they've gone. . . . We don't know nothin'. Not a thing.'

'He's right,' agreed Charlie Mint. 'But what I still don't figure is the 'why?' Why did they do what they did to Jed – and take nothin'? What was the real purpose of bein' out at the Newbutt spread?'

'That's easy,' said a youth, twanging his braces across his chest, 'Patsy was the reason. Any man here will agree if he's honest. Patsy's a fine-lookin' gal. One of the prettiest 'tween here and Walmscott. In fact, *the* prettiest. Them fellas wouldn't be able to resist her – 'specially not types like them. They take their women where they find 'em. But with Patsy they got real lucky. Bet they couldn't believe their eyes.'

'That's enough, young fella,' disciplined Pop Ryder, putting a flaring match to his pipe. 'T'ain't a savoury subject for discussion. We can all guess what Patsy's suffered.'

'Don't change the facts none,' persisted the youth, twanging his braces again.

'Well, if you ask me, I reckon them rats ain't more than

a dozen miles away,' piped a man from the corner table. 'I'll wager they're out there right now – mebbe just watchin', or worse, just waitin'.'

Lanky polished a glass with renewed vigour and wondered for a moment if he should mention the lone rider he was still sure he had seen at the livery. But what good would it serve? There was no one out there now; no one else had mentioned the man; no one, it seemed, had seen him save Lanky. No, he decided, there was no point. . . .

The saloon fell instantly quiet as a footfall sounded on the boardwalk and the 'wings creaked open wearily.

No point, thought Lanky. None at all. The man was here.

# CHAPTER SIX

He was tall, straight, with easy but powerful shoulders and limbs; quiet hands that lay relaxed at his sides across the bulge of twin Colts beneath his long coat. A broad-brimmed hat worn low against the wind and rain shadowed a weathered face; a scar, long and twisted, spread the length of his left cheek to disappear deep into his neck and chest. The eyes were blue, watchful, penetrating when the gaze settled, with an instant reaction to movement, however slight, wherever it happened. They would miss nothing.

Lanky replaced the gleaming glass, laid aside his cloth and waited for the stranger to approach. He was not mistaken. This was the man he had seen earlier.

The saloon lay in silence. No one spoke; no one moved. Pop Ryder blew a thin wisp of smoke from the dying glow of his ancient pipe. Cuts Bailey simply stared. Charlie Mint swallowed. The youth flexed his braces but held them steady, his gaze narrowing suspiciously on the newcomer.

'Mornin',' said Lanky, carefully. 'Not much of a day for travellin'.'

The man stayed silent but continued to stare, first at Lanky, then, without seeming to move his head, only his eyes, at the town men to his left and right. But if someone at his back had moved, Lanky had the chilling feeling that

31

the man would know.

'Come far?' asked Lanky, a forced smile flickering at his lips.

The man's gaze settled as if content for the moment that no threat lurked. 'This Random?' His voice had a dry, cutting edge to it, raw as the mountain wind.

'That's us, mister,' beamed Lanky, the smile relaxing naturally. 'T'ain't much, but it's home. Leastways, we like it. Scraped it out of the dirt way back. Ain't on the stage route yet, but we're hopeful. Who knows? Changin' world, ain't it?'

'Too darned fast for me,' piped Pop from behind a cloud of new smoke.

'Town have a sheriff?' asked the man.

Lanky's smile broadened again. 'You bet. Sheriff Caulk. Fine fella. One of the best. Keeps a close eye on matters. Ain't much escapes him.' He nodded in agreement with himself. 'Got a doc too. Doc Marchman. Another fine fella. Cuts Bailey there does the barberin' hereabouts. If it's horse tack you need, Charlie Mint's your man. And you'd go some way to better the selection at McKellan's store. Some stuff there from back East, if that's the sort of thing that interests you. T'ain't everybody who. . . .' Lanky's voice trailed away.

'Livery?' said the man, his gaze tightening.

The silence in the bar stiffened. Lanky swallowed, his fingers creeping nervously for the reassurance of the glass cloth. The man continued to stare, his eyes suddenly darker, concentrated, unblinking.

'Sure,' began Lanky, hesitantly. 'We got a livery. Smart place. Clean. Jed does. . . .' He checked himself. 'That is to say, Jed *did* a good job, knew his business. But he unfortunately . . . which is to say, not puttin' too fine a point on it—'

'He was murdered,' called a man from the corner table. 'Somebody hanged him, right there in his own corral. Just did it. No good reason. Left him hangin' there.'

The gathering murmured, shuffled feet, creaked chairs and shifted glasses. The stranger remained perfectly still, making no attempt to turn to the men at his back.

'And that ain't all,' called another voice. 'Some scum-bags killed two fellas at the Newbutt spread; shot clean through at point-blank range, then raped Elmer's daughter, Patsy. Doc Marchman'll tell you. He'll spell it out like it was.'

'Town ain't a very savoury place right now, mister,' offered the man at the corner table. 'Mebbe you'd best ride on.'

The stranger did not move. His gaze stayed fixed on Lanky's steadily weakening face that had the pallor now of his worn cloth.

'Sounds good advice to me, mister,' said a man closer to the bar, pushing back his limp-brimmed hat to scratch his balding head. 'I'd take it. I'd ride.'

Pop Ryder grunted. 'Don't look much to me like a fella who takes kindly to advice,' he muttered to himself between releasing clouds of smoke.

The man placed a hand on the bar. 'You got a room?' he asked.

Lanky swallowed again and buried his fingers in the glasscloth. 'Sure,' he answered, 'we got a room. Half-a-dozen come to that. You want a room?'

The man nodded.

'That'll be no problem. Number Four. Overlooks the street, but if you'd prefer a back—'

'Number Four will be fine.'

'Suit yourself,' said Lanky, forcing the smile into life. 'I'll just . . . didn't catch your name, mister.'

'Didn't give it.'

'No, o'course. Well, t'ain't of consequence. Don't need a name. You be stayin' long? One night, two, mebbe more? It don't make no difference, room ain't goin' no place, is it?'

'It depends,' said the man, taking the key that Lanky slid across the bar.

'You bet,' smiled Lanky. 'No problem. No hurry neither. Heck, who needs to hurry?' Lanky picked up the glasscloth as if collecting his courage. 'Enjoy your stay, mister. Anythin' you want, you just sing out. Yessir. You bet.'

The man had stepped away from the bar and was heading for the shadowy stairs to the upper floor, when the tense silence was broken by a twang of the youth's braces and the clipped, demanding tone of his voice.

'Hey, mister, you hold it there a minute.'

The man stopped but did not turn.

Twenty pairs of eyes settled on the stranger's back.

Pop Ryder blew smoke and muttered deep in his throat.

Cuts Bailey began to sweat. Charlie Mint was already sweating. Lanky screwed the glasscloth to a ball in his hands.

'I wanna ask you somethin',' clipped the youth in the same uncomprising tone.

The man remained still; appeared to sigh, then to turn slowly, silently, the folds of the long coat cruising round his legs like grey birds.

'Ask away,' said the man, his eyes settling in that dark unblinking stare.

The youth licked his lips as he hooked his thumbs dramatically into his braces and leered in his new-found attention. 'I wanna know,' he began, 'where you've been

34

these past few days. And that means *exactly* where you've been. Where've you come from; which trail you followed; where you could – and might – have stopped. I wanna know these things on account of how this town's seen some pretty nasty things these past hours and we ain't—'

'You through there, boy?' asked the man.

'I ain't no boy,' flared the youth, flexing his braces. 'I'm man enough to know how things are hereabouts, and I'm sure as hell not for takin'—'

The man moved forward, his firm steps across the wooden floor silencing the youth as if clamping his jaws shut, his stare fixed, penetrating, seeing into and perhaps through the young body ahead of him.

Lanky screwed the glasscloth tighter. Pop Ryder closed his eyes despairingly, but opened them instantly. The town men stood and sat transfixed.

The man came to within a pace of the youth, halted, stared and twitched his lips to a faint grin. The long scar on his cheek seemed to move. The youth said nothing as he began to sweat.

'Appreciate your problems, boy,' said the man, his tone steady, almost gentle. 'But, sorry, can't help you.' The grin eased to a full smile. 'Meantime . . .' The smile faded like a lost shadow as the man's right hand sprang forward, drew the youth's left brace to its full extent and released it with a force that thudded like a rock into the young man's chest. 'Meantime, I'm tired and would like to rest. All right?'

The youth fingered his bruised chest, swallowed, sweated. 'I was only. . . .' he croaked. But by then the man had turned, walked to the stairs and disappeared into the gloom

Pop Ryder blinked. 'That was close,' he wheezed behind a cloud of smoke. 'So sonofabitch close.'

# CHAPTER SEVEN

The stranger's arrival in town had served only to deepen Sheriff Caulk's already nagging headache. He had suffered a sleepless night, too preoccupied with the organization of his street patrol and keeping a check generally on the town homes and the folk in them to snatch at more than fitful dozing.

First light had done nothing to cheer his mood with Doc Marchman's news of what Patsy had managed to tell him. He was now resigned to the grim reality that four men – nameless, unknown, unsighted, but viciously ruthless – were embarked on a reign of terror against both his town and the outlying homesteads. And for no reason he could either see or begin to imagine. 'Madness,' he had muttered to himself more than once.

The rain and heavy cloud had darkened the outlook. There was a raw chill to the edge of the squalls that pummelled the town like a punch-drunk drifter. Where the wind howled and whined, grey ghosts seemed to moan. Or were they mocking?

And then Charlie Mint and Cuts Bailey had burst into his office with the news of the stranger's arrival at the Golden Gaze.

'I seen some mean characters in my time,' winked

36

Charlie. 'You bet to it. But this fella, he's *mean.*'

'Mean,' repeated Cuts. 'He's got the look. You know the look, Sheriff? That mean look.'

'And a scar,' added Charlie in his next breath. 'He didn't get that playin' Mister Nice-man. You can bet to that too.'

'Knifed,' said Cuts bluntly. 'Real bad.'

'So who is he?' asked Caulk.

Charlie crossed to the window and winced at the grey deserted, dripping street. 'Ain't said, and ain't likely to neither. He's that sort of fella.'

Cuts nodded. 'He's just here, Sheriff. Right here in Random, and I for one don't like the smell of it.'

Cuts and Charlie had no sooner left the office than Ben McKellan arrived.

'You've heard, I take it? About the stranger?'

Caulk assured him that he had. Strangers came and went, he reminded the storekeeper. It was in the nature of things. Men travelled. Arrived some place. Moved on. It was hardly a crime.

'Nor is it,' agreed Ben. 'Leastways, not in normal circumstances, but things ain't exactly normal here, are they? Far from it. Town folk are jumpy; suspicious, easily spooked. Strange face scares 'em. Only natural.'

'Well, the fella ain't committed no crime or broken any law hereabouts to my knowledge,' resolved Caulk. 'And that means he's free to come and go, rent a room for as long as he pleases. Don't see it no other way.'

Caulk had been careful not to mention the news of the four men described by Patsy. Charlie and Cuts would have spread the news faster than the wind whipping the rain; Ben McKellan's store would have buzzed with new rumour and speculation. And, in any case, Patsy had said so little.

No, he had decided, this was not the time. The town had its mystery stranger to keep it occupied. He was enough for now.

An hour later, as the sheriff eased his tired body into his long coat in preparation for a turn around the town, he was hailed from the boardwalk by an anxious-looking Lanky Joe.

'What's the trouble, Lanky?' frowned Caulk, joining the saloon proprietor in the relative dry of the boardwalk fronting his office. The wind whipped viciously at their coats. Rain sprayed wildly on the surge of the gusts. 'Don't tell me that stranger's givin' you trouble already.'

Lanky wiped the beading damp from his face, tipped rain from his hat, and narrowed his eyes against the piercing wind. 'No trouble,' he said, his voice fading in the teeth of a gust. 'Leastways, not back there in the saloon. No, it's just that I thought you should know I reckon I've seen this stranger before.'

'Oh?' said Caulk, putting a hand to his wind-threatened hat. 'And when was that?'

'Today. Early this mornin'.'

'You mean he was here in town?'

'At the livery. By the tree at the corral. He just sat there, watchin'.'

'Did he see you?' asked Caulk.

'Must have. I was the only one about, sweepin' as usual. Couldn't have missed me.'

'But he didn't approach?'

'No. Didn't move. Didn't wave – didn't do nothin'. Just sat. Watchin' or waitin', hard to say. Ben McKellan called across – and then the fella was gone. Nothin' of him 'til he walked into the saloon. Ben didn't see him. Did your men on patrol report anythin'?'

'Nothin',' pondered Caulk, turning his gaze to the still deserted street. 'So why, I wonder, was the fella there?'

'Who was he watchin'?' muttered Lanky. 'But suppose he was waitin'. Who was he waitin' for? And why?'

Caulk was reluctant to probe into the questions and relieved to be able to leave them with Lanky on the pretext of completing his patrol of the town. They parted company at the saloon, with the sheriff promising to look in at the end of his turn. He went on his way with only the wind and the lash of the rain for company.

But it was only a matter of time – a few brief minutes – before he was joined by the jostle of his thoughts. . . .

A cold, calculated hanging; a homestead massacre; a young woman taken to the brink of nightmare; four riders; a stranger in town. . . . All linked or strange coincidencies of time and place? Was the stranger one of the four, but if so why was he here? Or was he simply a stranger passing through? Where were the four men who had ridden onto the Newbutt spread? Would Patsy be able to remember and describe her ordeal in more detail? And if so. . . .

Sheriff Caulk had reached the livery and been welcomed into the dry and warmth of the old forge by Pete Phillips when he finally put aside his thoughts and concentrated on the fresh coffee offered.

'Seen anythin', anybody?' asked Caulk from behind the steaming brew.

'Nobody save the town fellas patrollin',' said Pete. 'Been a whole sight too busy to take much notice.'

'You need more help here?'

'I'm copin',' grinned Pete.

Caulk nodded. 'Keep your eyes peeled.' It was almost as an afterthought that he added, 'You seen anythin' of this stranger we got in town?'

'Heard talk of him, but he ain't set foot hereabouts. Not to my knowledge he ain't.'

But Lanky had sworn he had seen him, right there, beneath the tree in the livery corral. Maybe he had been mistaken.

It was mid-afternoon when Fisty Fox rode back to town from the Newbutt spread and reported immediately to the sheriff.

'Had this strange feelin' I wasn't alone out there,' mused Fisty. 'You know the feelin', like there was some-body there, not at your shoulder, but just there?'

'Spooky place to be right now,' said Caulk. 'Bad atmos-phere. Bad smells. No place for a fella on his own.'

'But that's the point,' persisted Fisty. 'I wasn't alone. There was somebody there. I saw him. Lone rider; some distance away, but there, sure enough. Just sat his horse, lookin', watchin'.

'Or waitin',' said Caulk.

'Waitin'? Waitin' for what?'

It was later, with the rain still steady but lighter, the wind still gusting and the street still grey in its emptiness, when Sheriff Caulk pulled on his coat again, left the office in the charge of Joe Dimes and headed in the direction of Doc Marchman's clapboard home on the south side of town.

He needed now to know more of the four men who had appeared at the Newbutt spread; needed desperately for Patsy to trawl her memory for the slightest thing that might give him a clue to their identity. Could she recall what they looked like? Had names, places been mentioned – anything, however seemingly remote or obscure, that might lead him to plan some response?

Hell, the town was jumpy enough as it was. Another death, more talk of lone riders, strangers in town – it only needed a spark to fire a powder-keg.

Patsy might have the answers.

He reached the front door and tapped quietly. No answer. He tapped again. Still nothing. He waited a moment, tapped again, this time with a bolder touch.

Maybe Doc was dozing. Could be he was tending Patsy. Maybe he should call later. But, hell, the rain was falling faster now, swirling on the whip of the wind. The light was fading. Only an hour or so, he guessed, to dusk.

He placed his hand on the doorknob, turned it slowly and eased the door open, at the same time removing his hat and squinting into the gloom of the main living-room.

'Doc?' he called quietly. 'Doc, you about? It's me, Sheriff Caulk. I was just wonderin'. . . .'

He closed the door behind him and moved deeper into the room. He squinted ahead and frowned. Why no sounds? Why no lights, not even a single lantern? He halted, his right hand dropping instinctively to the butt of his holstered Colt.

And then he could feel it – a presence. Close. Somewhere to his left.

His fingers tightened on the Colt.

'I wouldn't if I were you,' said the voice.

A gun hammer clicked in the dark.

# CHAPTER EIGHT

The sweat trickled cold as ice down Sheriff Caulk's neck. He stiffened, flicked his eyes to the left, probing for the shape behind the voice. 'Who in hell are you and what are you doin' here?'

Silence. Caulk peered closer. Now he could see two eyes; bright blue eyes that simply stared, unblinking but with a sharpness that seemed to mock.

'I said who—?' began Caulk.

'We heard you, mister,' grated a voice ahead of him.

The sheriff's eyes widened only to narrow again in the sudden flare of a lantern primed on the table in the centre of the room. He swallowed. The man facing him was lean, tall, with a dark, pitted face, hooked nose hanging like a craggy outcrop of rock over his thin lips. He looked grubby; smelled it too, thought Caulk.

His gaze shifted to the man to his left. The blue eyes were still staring, still unblinking in the face of a much younger, cleaner-shaven fellow, with lank, corn-coloured hair sprouting like scrub from beneath his hat. He grinned and ran a finger over the barrel of the Colt lazing in his lap.

'Where's Doc?' croaked Caulk. 'And Patsy? If you've—'

'Ease up there, Sheriff,' quipped the hook-nosed man,

leaning forward into the glow of the lantern. 'They ain't come to no harm – leastways not yet they ain't.'

The younger man's grin broadened to a smile. 'S'right. They're right here. In there.' He glanced towards the room where Doc had been nursing Patsy. The smile faded. 'Time you slipped that gunbelt to the floor, Sheriff. It fidgets me to see guns in other men's belts.'

Caulk mouthed a silent curse, gazed for a moment into hook nose's dark eyes, and cleared the gunbelt from his waist. 'I'm still waitin' to hear—' he began again.

'All in good time, Sheriff, all in good time. We ain't in no hurry.' The hook-nosed man permitted himself a thin grin across his mean lips. 'And you ain't goin' no place right now. So you just pull up that chair there and settle yourself. All right?'

'Just who the hell are you fellas?' grated Caulk, his throat drying to a parched creek bed.

The wind gusted at the window spattering it with rain.

'Me,' said hook-nose, 'I'm Bullets Machin. Fella sittin' there is Keefer Drone, and the boss, Edrow Scoone and our other partner, Halfneck Quire, are in the room along of Doc and that pretty young filly we crossed back there at the spread.'

The sweat iced over in Caulk's neck. 'You were the scum who. . . .' His voice cracked. 'Mark my words, mister, you'll hang for what you did to that gal and her kin. Hang, damn you, and that'll be too good—'

'Yeah, yeah, I'm sure. Heard it said a hundred times,' said Machin, leaning back from the lantern glow. 'But right now—'

The door to the bedroom opened and Doc Marchman stumbled into the light ahead of a man with what seemed like a permanent scowl on his weathered, trail-streaked face and small snaky eyes set close. Dirt and dust drifted from his clothes like blown mist.

'Name's Scoone,' said the man, fixing his stare on Caulk. 'You heard of me?'

'Never,' said Caulk, eyeing the thickening bruise on Doc's cheek.

'Good,' grinned Scoone. 'That's what I like to hear. Me and the boys ain't for bein' known, 'specially now we've found our new home, so to speak. Somewhere we plan on stayin'.'

Doc closed his eyes and shook his head despondently.

Caulk's swallow across his dry throat stung like a bite. 'And what in hell is that supposed to mean?' he groaned.

Scoone walked slowly round the table, the fingertips of his right hand tracing a track as he went. He halted, grinned and fixed Caulk with a dark stare. 'It means, mister, that me and my partners are takin' over your town. We're goin' to settle here, live here, eat, sleep and drink here – and help ourselves to your womenfolk when we take a fancy – and generally have ourselves a quiet, untroubled life for just as long as it suits, which right now looks like bein' indefinitely.' His grin spread, wet and lopsided into the stubble that had thickened round his mouth. 'You got a problem with that?' he added.

Caulk was conscious of eyes watching him, of a suddenly deeper silence filling the room. Doc Marchman had turned physically greyer as if shouldering time itself. Bullets Machin leaned forward again into the glow of the lantern; Keefer Drone smoothed a finger down the barrel of his nursed Colt, and now the fourth man, Halfneck Quire, had sauntered to the open door of the bedroom to lounge untidily on the jamb.

'You lost your tongue, Sheriff?' quipped Scoone.

'Mebbe he ain't much for the idea,' grinned Drone.

'Well, ain't that goin' to be a shame!' murmured Machin, his eyes glinting in the lantern glow.

'Real shame,' echoed Drone.

'They hanged Jed,' blurted Doc, sweat beading freely on his brow.

Caulk stiffened, his blood cold in his veins, stifled a shudder and licked his lips.

'Hey, now, ease up there,' said Scoone. 'I ain't for trouble at this point. Sheriff here will read the situation well enough. He looks a sensible sort of fella. Spell it out to him, Bullets. Tell the man the nature of our business.'

'A pleasure,' smiled Machin, his glare darkening. 'Keepin' it brief, we take what we want where we find it. And sometimes, on special occasions, we make a real special effort and go lookin for it.'

Keefer Drone tittered. 'Like we did at that homestead, eh?'

'Just like that,' continued Machin. 'It's been like that for some years, mainly up the far north which is mebbe why you ain't heard of us.' He drummed his dirt-grained fingers on the tabletop. 'But now things are changin'. We're lookin for a place to rest up long-term – mebbe permanently. Somewhere we ain't to go lookin' or scratchin' for our needs. Some place where we're provided for, looked after real sensitive, and with respect. And guess what, Sheriff – we've chosen your neat little town.'

Machin leaned back from the light glow and spread his arms wide. 'Now ain't that some honour? Imagine, of all the towns in all the territories any which-way you care to ride, Random gets to be chosen by Edrow Scoone and his long-standin' partners as the one place they care to call home. A place to settle down. Imagine!'

The four men laughed among themselves. Doc shook his head again and tried to bury a trembling hand in the pocket of his pants. Caulk swallowed and winced at the sting in his throat. Sweat trickled freely down his back.

Machin raised a hand for silence. ' 'Course,' he began again, 'we ain't no fools. There was a good chance you might not take too kindly to our arrival. Oh, yes, a good chance, human nature bein' what it is. So, just to make sure you understand how serious we are – and what it might mean to resist – we left an early warning: the fella at the livery, the gal here and them poor souls you must have discovered by now at the homestead.'

Scoone took a slow turn round the room, all eyes following him as he passed into and out of the shadows. 'We can be mean, Sheriff. Real mean. Mess with us and you'll find out. More hangin's, more bodies . . . they don't give us no sleepless nights. But, show a welcomin' attitude and you'll have a town under our personal protection. Guaranteed.'

He halted, the rain and wind still swirling on the night, the lantern glow flickering for a moment across his face to mottle it with patches of shadow.

'So, what's your reckonin', Sheriff: you goin' to make us at home here in Random, or do we finish the young gal there with a dozen or so of your worthy citizens joinin' her? Choice is yours.'

# CHAPTER NINE

'Nightmare. T'ain't nothin' else. Can't say other. It's just a nightmare.'

Storekeeper Ben McKellan mopped his brow with a freshly laundered bandanna that still carried a hint of soapy scent, wiped the rim of his hat and set it firmly back on his head.

He glanced round the faces of the men who had been forced under threat of the death of Patsy Newbutt, and almost certainly others, to gather in the Golden Gaze saloon. He glanced at the clock above the rows of bottles on the shelves behind Lanky's bar. Hell, he thought, the night had not yet reached seven and life in Random had been turned on its head. His brow began to bead with sweat again, but he resisted another swirl of the bandanna.

'We're goin' to be prisoners in our own town,' said Cuts Bailey vacantly.

'And them scumbags ain't goin' to pay a cent for a thing,' added Charlie Mint equally vacantly. 'Not a thing. . . .'

'Mebbe we should get to doin' somethin' right now, before the rats get a real hold,' grunted the storekeeper.

'They've got a hold,' said Fisty Fox. 'They've got Patsy. And believe me, they'd finish her soon as spit.'

'Mebbe we're goin' to have to bide our time. Trust to the sheriff and Doc there.' Joe Dimes ran a hand over his itchy stubble. 'Anybody here lifts a gun against them rats and that'll be another body.'

The men fell silent. All eyes in the crowded saloon were watching Doc Marchman and two bar girls help a pale-faced Patsy Newbutt up the creaking stairs to the room where Scoone had ordered she was to be held. 'And nobody – but nobody save Doc here – goes near her. You hear me? Not one step. First man does and I'll hang him right there in the street, jut like we did that livery fella. And this time the body'll stay there 'til it rots.'

Scoone's glare round the silent saloon had been dark, wet with a sweat that oozed threat and menace. This fellow enjoys killing, Caulk had thought; he relishes the prospect of taking a life in the meanest, cruellest way he can devise and letting it brood its own fear. And his sidekicks' guns were there to ensure he ruled without question and completely unchallenged.

But why Random, he had pondered, when he, Doc and Patsy had been marched from Doc's home to the saloon? Chance; simply bad luck? Might it just as easily have been any other town? But one thing was for sure, they had watched the place closely, observed its patterns of life, even known the layout and had invaded Doc's home with ease.

Now it seemed their intentions had been equally well planned: they would take over the town, be the law – the only law; Scoone's law – for as long as they wished; take whatever they needed; kill when challenged – and hold Patsy Newbutt hostage in an upstairs room at the Golden Gaze until it suited them to do other. No straight thinking man would dare raise a hand against any one of the four, not if he wanted to stay breathing.

Sheriff Caulk and Doc Marcham had trudged through the wet night like men in a daze of bewilderment, disbelief, confusion – and not least seething but imprisoned anger.

'You men here listen up real close,' Scoone ordered from where he stood at the bar, Bullets Machin to his right, Keefer Drone and Halfneck Quire to his left.

'Movement round here is goin' to be tight from here on. Anybody leaves town, their kin will pay – with their lives. Anybody tryin' to leave town who gets caught will be strung up. Anybody raisin' a gun, a blade or anythin' I reckon to be a weapon will be bull-whipped – then strung up. I ain't much for blazin' lead, 'ceptin' where necessary, but I sure as hell appreciate a good hangin'!'

Scoone's smile broke across his face like the sudden appearance of a fissure in pitted rock. His eyes glinted, shifting quickly from left to right, missing nothing among the town men. Bullets Machin scratched his nose; Drone smoothed a finger over the butt of his Colt; Quire hawked and looked round for a spittoon.

Young Jessie Brown standing at the front of the gathering, stepped forward, his face flushed on a mixture of anger and three swift measures of cheap whiskey. 'We ain't for givin' up our freedom just like that, mister, whoever you are or think you are. Same goes for our town. Hell, most of us here helped build the place, scratchin' it out of the dirt. If you think. . . .'

Caulk winced as he saw what was coming.

Cuts Bailey joined the general chorus of groans. Charlie Mint and Pop Ryder sank the dregs in their empty glasses. The town men fell to a chilled silence. A bar girl shivered and accepted the comfort of the nearest arm.

It was Halfneck Quire who moved clear of Scoone's side to within inches of Jessie's sweat-soaked face.

Quire stared for a moment, unblinking, silent save for the hiss of his fetid breath through chipped, yellowing teeth, then slowly, deliberately drew his Colt from his holster and struck the barrel across Jessie's left cheek to leave a deep gash.

Blood ran freely into his neck, some spilling to the floor, but he remained standing, defiant and still flushed.

'You wanna make an issue, fella?' slurred Quire.

Jessie raised trembling fingers to the bleeding gash. 'I was only tryin' to say—'

Quire raised the Colt again. Jessie began to duck, but this time there was no thud of the barrel into flesh. This time Quire fired – a single, pinpoint shot into the centre of Jessie's forehead.

As the echoing drone of the shot faded, a deeper, colder silence crept in from the dark, wet street like a bedraggled animal. Sheriff Caulk's head was spinning. Cuts Bailey sweated. Charlie and Pop Ryder had dropped their glasses to the floor at the shuddering blast of the shot.

Lanky Joe thought, not for the first time that night, that he had seen the stranger bar-side of the 'wings only seconds before Quire had raised his Colt. Now, there was no one there. The man came and went like the mist.

'Get that mess out of here,' shouted Scoone. 'And let that be another lesson to you – all of you: Don't get lippy with us. It always ends in a mess.' He sank a measure of whiskey, banged the glass back on the bar and reached for the fresh bottle prepared by Lanky.

'Keep it comin', fella,' he grinned. 'Keep it comin'.

Night's young yet – so we'll make this our settlin' in party, eh? Why not? Edrow Scoone's found home – and brought his family with him!'

In the next few hours the folk of Random reeled from nightmare to brutal reality, half expecting at any moment to wake and discover Scoone and his sidekicks had been no more than ogres in a bad dream. But there was no waking. The rain-soaked night, the crowded saloon, the blood-smeared boards where the young man had been shot, the sight of Scoone drifting ever deeper into alcoholic haze, the cowering girls, the bewildered men, these were the reality.

Sheriff Caulk did his best to persuade the town men to return home to their families. 'There ain't no more to be done here, fellas,' he had counselled. 'Best get some rest, eh? Tomorrow's another day.'

'Goin' to have to do somethin', somehow, ain't we, Sheriff?' a man had urged. 'Can't just sit back and let this happen, can we?'

Perhaps not, Caulk had pondered later, when the saloon had finally cleared, Scoone and his men settled themselves at a table, the street returned to its silent emptiness, and he, Doc Marchman, Ben McKellan and Pop Ryder retired to sample a private drink in the sheriff's office.

'There'll be some hot-heads out there, you can bet to it,' said the storekeeper, sampling a measure of whiskey. 'And men will get killed. It's as certain as sun-up.'

'I'll do the best I can to keep things steady 'til we can do some more figurin', but, hell, it ain't goin' to be easy.' Caulk stared into his drink for a moment, then at the dark rain-streaked window.

'Damnit, nobody's expectin' you to keep a hold single-handed,' said Doc. 'We're all in this together, but we'll get nowhere – and only pile up the misery – if we get to blunderin' around like crazed steers. Them scum back there will kill instantly, indiscriminately, anybody, anywhere, men, women, mebbe even the young 'uns . . . they won't be fussed. They're here and they ain't for bein' shifted.'

Pop puffed gently on a corncob pipe. 'What have they run from?' he frowned. 'They pulled off some massive bank raid some place? Murdered somebody real important?'

'Or mebbe they've just got tired of runnin',' added Caulk, squinting through the window. 'Mebbe this is their end-of-the-line. A place to bury themselves.'

'Types like that Keefer Drone don't get to hidin' themselves away,' said McKellan. 'You seen the look in his eyes? He's for action; a meal of it. And regular. Same goes for that rat Quire. Shot young Jessie back there in the saloon without batting an eye.'

The four listened to a fresh gust of rain squalling like a bad cough along the boardwalk.

'Weather don't help none,' observed Caulk, moving closer to the window.

Pop Ryder released a thicker cloud of smoke. 'Anybody see anythin' of that stranger?' he asked almost casually.

'Seems like he got forgotten in all that's happened,' said McKellan. 'Mebbe he locked himself in his room and ain't moved since.'

'No, he didn't do that. Definitely not.' Doc finished his drink. 'Machin inspected all the rooms over the bar before I settled Patsy. If the fella had been there, Machin would have shifted him, you can bet to it.'

Pop tamped the tobacco in the bowl of his corncob. 'So where'd he go?'

The night wind gusted another swirl of rain.

# CHAPTER TEN

Lanky Joe could not sleep. Did not want to sleep would have been nearer the truth. There was too much happening – a whole heap too much already had – and now, along with most town folk, his confusion had exhausted him.

But not to the point of sleeping. Nossir! Just about everything in the Golden Gaze needed to be watched, including the private rooms. If only he could get near them. Bullets Machin was taking care of that. He was allowing no one – save his own type, the bar girls and Doc Marchman – to set so much as a foot on the stairs. A fine state of affairs in your own business, Lanky had grumbled inwardly, mulling over yet another scheme to sidestep Machin's guard. Not yet, it seemed, but there would come a time, that one chance. . . .

He sighed and began yet again to clean the saloon, polish glasses, shift things here, there and back again. Anything to beat the creeping tiredness that would sooner or later. . . . He shook his head. No sleeping; it would never be more than a fitful doze anyway, from which he would wake in a lathering sweat with doubtless one of the scumbags helping himself from the till, or worse the safe in the back room.

Sleeping was out!

Time instead to reckon other things. The stranger in town for one. He had definitely left his room before the arrival of Scoone and his men, and Pete Phillips had reported to Lanky that his horse was no longer at the livery, though he had not personally seen the stranger leave with the mount.

'Must've crept in real quiet, saddled up and moved out, soft as a shadow.' Pete had said. 'So what's with the fella? He get spooked or somethin'?'

That was as likely an explanation as any, Lanky had thought. Maybe he had seen Scoone and his men sneaking through town to Doc's home. Or maybe he had seen Scoone bringing Sheriff Caulk, Doc and Patsy to the Golden Gaze at gunpoint. Maybe he had just figured the whole set-up not for him and pulled out.

And who could blame him? Most fellows would do the same – though he might have settled his bill for the time he had been here. Lanky shrugged behind another flourish of the glasscloth. Hell, you win some, you lose some. . . . But the situation here right now was definitely on the downside of loss.

He glanced round the dimly lit saloon. All the town men, together with Doc Marchman and the sheriff had left. Scoone had staggered upstairs in search of a bar girl, leaving the sidekicks in charge: Keefer Drone at a table polishing the barrel of his Colt, Halfneck Quire pacing remorselessly across the batwings, his stare fixed on the rain and wind buffeted empty street, and Machin guarding the stairs.

There had been no banter, no conversation between the three. In fact, they barely seemed aware of the others' presence, and only occasionally Lanky's as he went about his bar business. If half-a-dozen determined town men were to burst in now, Colts and rifles blazing, and if they kept the lead flying for five minutes, this whole miserable mess might—

'Hey, fella,' called Drone, waving his gun loosely in Lanky's direction, 'how about you brewin' up some nice sweet coffee for me and my partners here? Throat gets kinda parched this time of day, don't you reckon? So you goin' to oblige, fella?' The Colt spun dazzlingly on one finger.

'Sure,' said Lanky, laying aside the glasscloth. 'Got some fresh beans outback. Give me a couple of minutes.'

He primed a lantern and moved through the shadowy gloom to the back door, opened it and stepped into the cold night air. Rain still swirled and danced on the wind as he crossed to the supplies shed and for some reason – perhaps the flicker of another light, a sound – paused with the key in his fingers about to unlock the door.

He raised the lantern for a better view ahead and peered towards the line of an old rickety fence that had once enclosed Billy Speck's prize hogs. And once again, just as before, he was not mistaken.

The man mounted astride the horse there was the same fellow he had watched at the livery; the same man who had walked into his saloon that very day, taken a room and then disappeared. Except that he had not gone anywhere. He was right here. Still in Random.

Why?

The rain eased slowly through that long dark night. Lanky Joe brewed coffee; watched Scoone's men booze and doze; listened to the wind through the street, the creaks and groans of doors and timbers.

Ben McKellan slept for what might have been an hour,

but seemed like minutes; paced his living-room; paced his store; watched the street from windows and, like Lanky, listened to the wind.

Cuts Bailey and Charlie Mint emptied a bottle of whiskey between them in Charlie's gloomy back room and discussed the situation that had developed from every angle they could imagine. They came to no conclusion and got nowhere, so they too got to watching the street and listening to the wind.

Pop Ryder and a handful of town men without settled homes and waiting wives gathered round the warmth and comfort of the livery forge where young Pete Phillips brewed endless pots of coffee while keeping watch over the stabled horses.

Some men were all for hatching a plot to rid the town of Scoone and his sidekicks come sun-up. They considered whether they could maybe sneak up on the scum while they slept; or maybe create a diversion that would scatter them from the saloon to be picked off one by one like the rats they were.

How about trying to poison them? had been one suggestion. Maybe Lanky could sprinkle something on their food, or fix their drink in some way. Doc would know what to use.

Or would it be better, and a whole sight safer, for somebody to ride out and fetch help. How long would that take? Where would the fellow ride to? Supposing Scoone found out. What then?

Perhaps the bar girls could get the sonsofbitches so drunk, so helpless, completely at their mercy that—

But, hell, it was all apple pie in the sky. Fact of it was that very little could be done – and even if there was, who would do it? Who would have the guts, the skills, the know-how?

Or would it be wiser to trust to Sheriff Caulk? When all was said and done, he was the law around here, he wore the badge and carried the fastest gun they knew. Maybe they should all get behind him. Do as he said and follow whatever plan he had in mind. Assuming he had one.

Pop Ryder contributed very little to the discussions. He seemed content enough to smoke his corncob, listen to the talk, watch the night and listen to the wind. His only contribution was to wonder where in hell that stranger might be holed up on a night like this.

Doc Marchman dozed in the quiet of his home and woke constantly in a beaded sweat that felt as cold as mountain ice.

His mind had long since ceased to reel; images no longer flashed like sudden lightning, and his thoughts had passed from a jumble to a fixed, focused objective: he was the only man in town with unquestioned access to Patsy Newbutt. And it was in Patsy that there might lie an answer to Edrow Scoone's threatened reign of tyranny.

An idea – not yet formulated to a plan – was taking shape. It would be dangerous; selected folk would have to be trusted to the very limits. There might be a loss – some-body might, perhaps certainly would, get killed – but the result would be worth one life to save a town and the dozens of lives within it.

But it was still too early, too soon, for Doc to be reck-oning on details. He needed to talk to the sheriff, to Lanky Joe and two, maybe three of the bar girls.

Meantime, there was the night, the rain and the wind.

Like Doc, Sheriff Caulk could only doze, pace his office and, from time to time as the night wore on, step out to the boardwalk and scan what he could see of the street.

There was still a low light in the Golden Gaze, but little

movement, save for the occasional appearance of Keefer Drone, or Halfneck Quire, taking in the fresher air.

Twice he had reckoned a single shot from a steady Winchester would take out one or other of the rats. But twice he had been forced to admit that the cost of that single shot would be horrendous. He had abandoned the notion and gone back to simply watching the rain begin to ease, the street puddles to stand unmoving, the wind to die and eventually, as first light slipped in and the earth began to warm, a mist to lift like breath.

It hung thick as a shroud when the shot rang out and a girl screamed.

# CHAPTER ELEVEN

Nobody in Random failed to hear the shot or the scream. As the echoes died away they sat, stood, lay exactly where they were as if the sounds had been a signal for them to freeze.

It was a full minute before Sheriff Caulk was heading along the mist-shrouded street in the direction of the Golden Gaze, his mind teeming with images, possibilities, grisly details. Did he already know what he would find? Had he seen it, rehearsed it, a dozen times in his head? Were shootings, dead bodies, blood, inevitable wherever Scoone and his sidekicks reined in?

The swish of Lanky Joe's besom on the boardwalk fronting the saloon had been the town's waking call for years. Was it about to be replaced by gunshots and screams?

Ben McKellan stood alone outside his store as Caulk strode past him. 'Came from the saloon, I reckon,' he murmured. 'Didn't see nothin'. Ain't slept any. You sleep any, Sheriff?'

Caulk merely grunted and kept moving.

Charlie Mint, Pop Ryder and Cuts Bailey were making their careful way from the livery. Three town men were gathered opposite the saloon. A girl at a window in the room above Charlie's saddlery hugged herself in a blanket and blinked the sleep from her eyes. A dog sloped away down an alley, ears flattened, tail between its legs.

Doc Marchman had reacted instinctively to the shot. He was into his jacket, had collected his bag, settled his hat and slammed the door on the quiet clapboard home within thirty seconds.

Fisty Fox stepped to his side as Doc passed the sheriff's office. 'Might've known,' he grunted, falling into Doc's pace while still adjusting his belt. 'Time of day ain't of no consequence to types like them rats. Hell, is this goin' to be the way of things, Doc? It's goin' to be like walkin' on hot coals.'

'Let's wait, Fisty. We ain't seen nothin' yet. Mebbe it was just an accident. Just 'cus a shot gets loosed don't mean to say—'

Doc's words died on him at the creak of the saloon 'wings and the appearance on the boardwalk of Halfneck Quire, a soft cynical sneer on his lips to greet Sheriff Caulk.

'No need to fret none, Sheriff,' he quipped, the fingers of his right hand drumming lightly over the butt of his holstered Colt. 'One of them bar gals, name of Annie, got a touch out of hand.'

'If you've—' began Caulk.

'No, no, she ain't dead. Just been taught a lesson. She'll get over it soon enough.' He turned to peer into the misty street. 'Ah – here's Doc. Right on time. Ain't that fortunate? Real service. Couldn't be better.' He grinned. 'Nice town you've got here, Sheriff. Credit to you. Sure as hell glad we found it.'

'I want to see the gal,' demanded Caulk. 'Right now.'

Quire's grin faded. 'Don't reckon that'll be possible.

Boss ain't about yet. Tends to sleep in some, 'specially when he's got warm company snugglin' up.' He winked. 'Know what I mean?'

'I couldn't give a damn about Scoone,' seethed Caulk, clenching his fists as his colour rose. 'I'm the law here, and I—'

'Don't push your luck, Sheriff,' clipped Quire, his fingers tightening on the Colt. 'Just let the Doc through there. That's it. And tell them starin' town folk back of you to get about their business. You hear me? So get to it, eh? Then come back when we're good and ready for you. I make myself clear?'

Caulk's face had darkened like a cloud. The mist moved about the street and round the watching town men as if to hide them. No one said another word.

'Did you see that? Did you hear that sonofabitch; the way he mouthed like he did to Sheriff Caulk? Damn it, I thought for a split-second there the sheriff would get to spoilin' for a stand up fight.'

The burly town man hitched his pants over a generous gut and left his thumbs hooked into the waistband. The others gathered round him at the back of Ben McKellan's store nodded and murmured their agreement, their breath rising like deeper clouds across the still clinging morning mist.

'Sheriff wouldn't do nothing like that,' said Cuts Bailey. 'Too much at stake.'

'I ain't so sure,' mused Charlie Mint, scratching across an irritation in his stubble. 'Sometimes a fella can get pushed a mite too far. Them rats are tryin' Caulk's patience. And they'll keep pushin' him. How far will he go before he snaps? I wouldn't wager a deal on that.'

'Me neither,' piped a tall, freckle-faced youth at the back of the gathering. 'Every man's got a breakin' point.'

'And what would you know about that, boy?' grinned Pop Ryder from his perch on an empty crate. He puffed a stream of smoke from his corncob. 'Since when have you been an expert on breakin' points?'

'I see what I see, feel what I feel,' quipped the youth, stretching himself to his full skinny height. 'Rate we're goin' here there ain't goin' to be no town for folk to get sore over, anyhow. Them scumbags'll clear the place. Drive 'em out if they ain't already shot 'em. Me, I'm for doin' somethin'. Damnit, if we don't we might as well—'

'Now, now, Billy,' soothed an older man at the youth's side. 'No need to get yourself hot-collared there. We all feel the same, 'course we do, but there's got to be a right way at the right time, and t'ain't no use sayin' other. Time will come—'

'But supposin' it don't,' persisted the youth. 'Supposin' there ain't never goin' to be this *right way, right time* business. What then? We just sit around waitin' to get shot, or hanged, or whatever? Hell, we might as well do ourselves a favour and finish it right now. Why not, eh? Save a whole lot of trouble, wouldn't it?'

'That's fool talk, boy, and you know it,' said Pop behind a thickening cloud of smoke. 'First man who draws on any one of Scoone's men is a dead man. He wouldn't get to loosin' a shot. Them fellas are professionals; killers through and through. One more life, one more body ain't goin' to count a jot by their reckoning. And that's the truth of it.'

'Well, mebbe we'll see about that.'

The youth had pulled clear of the gathering, one eye on a route from the back of the store to the deserted street.

'Now don't you go doin' nothin' stupid, Billy Jay,' urged Charlie Mint. 'That's big talk you're mouthin' there – but talk comes cheap, son, 'specially in circumstances like we got here. So just you simmer down, eh? Leave this to wiser heads. I'm sure the sheriff and Doc Marchman will think of somethin'. . . .'

But by then the youth had turned his back on the town men and disappeared into the mist.

'He got a gun?' asked Cuts Bailey.

'No,' piped a man, 'but he darn soon will have if we don't stop him!'

The men moved away like flies from a rippled pond, some to the right, some to the left, others to the nearest alley, all heading for the street.

'I'll go get the sheriff,' said Charlie.

'And if you see Doc, bring him too,' murmured Pop. 'I got a feelin' we'll be needin' him.'

Lanky Joe paused in his slow, rhythmic polishing of a saloon table and listened carefully. Something was happening out there in the street. He could hear muffled voices, footfalls through the many muddy pools of rainwater. A crowd was gathering. Town men? This early?

He stepped closer to the batwings and peered into the misty morning. He could see vague, blurred shapes. Bodies. Men seeming to come from all directions. Four there. Another three. He recognized Cuts Bailey. Pop Ryder. And now Ben McKellan was on the boardwalk fronting his store.

Lanky craned to get a view to his left. More men. Maybe half a dozen. Pete Phillips on his way from the livery. He craned to the right. Heck, now Sheriff Caulk was striding down the street, Charlie Mint and Fisty Fox in his wake.

What was going on?

Hold it, here was that mouthy youth, Billy Jay, dancing about like he had boots full of burrs. Now what in the name of reason was a hot-blooded type like him doing in a situation like this? Damn it, Billy Jay was just about capable of—

'So what's the big attraction?' grunted Halfneck Quire at Lanky's shoulder. He came closer to the 'wings. 'Oh, my, do I see what I think I see? My, my . . . I do believe we have a fancy upstart gunslinger headin' our way.' He turned to gaze deeper into the saloon. 'Hey, Keefer, stir your lazy butt. Come and see what we've got here.'

Keefer Drone sauntered casually to Quire's side, blinked on the flat grey light and scanned what could be seen of the street in a slow, steady movement that seemed to soak in the scene as it went.

'Well, ain't this goin' to be just dandy?' grinned Drone, skimming his fingers across the butt of his Colt. 'Early mornin' entertainment.' He placed a hand on Lanky's shoulder. 'Now you be a good fella and go fetch me a long measure of that best whiskey you keep back of the bar there. And one for my partner. We prefer to do our shootin' on a full stomach!'

# CHAPTER TWELVE

'Put that gun down, Billy. Right now! Down, I say!'

Sheriff Caulk's voice grated across the still morning air like a boot heel scraping rock. White breath poured from his mouth and slunk away to the mist as if to be anonymous. 'You hear me there, Billy? I'll blow that piece right out of your hand if I have to. Don't tempt me. I ain't for bein' messed with.'

Billy Jay stamped his stance in the mud to the right of the boardwalk fronting the Golden Gaze and broadened the crazed smile across his freckled face. His eyes widened, bright as stars as he twirled a Colt through his fingers, almost dropped it, and gathered it into a fumbled hold.

'Billy, I ain't for sayin' this again,' called Caulk, 'but if you don't—'

'Leave the boy be,' snapped Keefer Drone, brushing through the saloon 'wings to the boardwalk. 'Darn me if he don't look somewhat promisin'. Fair sport on a dull day. What do you reckon there, partner?'

Halfneck Quire followed through the 'wings to Drone's side, let the creak of worn hinges subside, spat into the mud and scratched his backside. 'All yours, my friend, all yours. He ain't no deal for the likes of me.'

Billy Jay stiffened his stand in the street mud and glared.

The town men hugging the boardwalks fell silent.

Lanky Joe stared over the 'wings from the bar like a startled hawk.

Cuts Bailey shivered; Charlie Mint blinked and began to sweat; Pop Ryder let the glow in his pipe die a natural death.

'Listen up, Billy,' called Caulk again. 'I ain't for findin' the breath too many times to say this, but I'm urgin' you now, this very minute to put that gun aside and step over here real calm. Ain't no harm done yet. We can all forget this. . . . It didn't happen. . . . All you gotta do is—'

'Hey, hold on there, Sheriff,' snapped Drone again. 'Let the boy speak for himself. Go ahead, son, say what you gotta say. Halfneck and me here are all ears. Just you speak up. That's a civil right. Ain't that so, Sheriff?'

Caulk bristled as he bit back a stream of mumbled curses. Fisty Fox's guts rumbled deep into his bowels.

The street lay in frozen, mist-filled silence.

'Well, I guess the sheriff agrees,' grinned Drone, 'even though he's a mite shy in expressin' himself. So speak up, boy. Let's be hearin' you loud and clear.'


Billy Jay tightened his grip on his Colt. His smile flickered uncertainly for a moment as he tried to shift his stance in the thickening mud. His right boot stuck firm. Water oozed from beneath the sole. He tried again. This time the left boot sank, oozing and gurgling water as it settled.

Billy's sudden panic showed in his wild glances, first at Scoone's sidekicks watching from the saloon's boardwalk, then at Sheriff Caulk, Fisty Fox and the gathering groups of town men, their faces grey with the dawning realization that Billy was stuck.

And his situation was worsening with every effort he made to free himself.

'Oh, my. . . . Oh, my,' sighed Pop Ryder, clamping the corncob tight between his chipped, broken teeth.

'He's makin' it worse,' murmured Fisty, wiping sweat from his brow.

'We should go help him,' said Cuts Bailey.

'Don't move. Don't nobody move,' urged Charlie Mint. 'We're only a spit short of a bloodbath.'

Ben McKellan closed the door to his store with a click that seemed as loud as a crack of lightning.

Alice, one of the older bar girls came close to Lanky Joe's side and snuggled her fingers into his hand. 'I'm scared,' she shivered, closing on Lanky's warmer body.

Lanky squeezed her hand in his. 'Me too, gal. We all are. Only natural.'

'When will it end?' whispered the girl.

'I ain't got an answer to that, my dear. But it will. It will. You'll see.'

The girl shuddered again. 'Can I tell you somethin', Mr Joe?' she murmured.

'Sure you can. You always can. Hell, you know that. Hey . . . if one if them rats has been—'

'No, no, it's not that. We can handle scum. No, it's about that stranger. You know, the one who walked in here, took a room, then – presto – vanished. Well, he ain't; he's close. I seen him.'

'When?' asked Lanky, shepherding the girl away from the batwings into the deserted saloon.

'This mornin'. About an hour or so ago.'

'Where?'

'I've got that room at the back. Number Five. Well, I

just kinda looked out. No reason. I just did. And there he was. Watchin'. His eyes movin' left to right, back again, like he was takin' everythin' in; seein' where things were. Well, that's what it seemed like to me.'

'He see you?' frowned Lanky.

'Don't think so. Didn't seem to. Coupla minutes later he was gone. Just like that.'

Lanky considered for a moment. He glanced at the 'wings and the street beyond them, then at the saloon, the stairs to the upper rooms. 'Doc still with Patsy and Annie?'

The girl nodded. 'Annie's doin' fine. Them rats scared her more than anythin'.'

Lanky grunted. 'Well, you get to him and tell him what you saw. All right? And keep away from these 'wings. There's goin' to be some lead flyin' any minute now. . . .'

'Hey, boy, you plannin' on spendin' the day there or do you want a helpin' hand?' Keefer Drone's grin widened until he was tittering quietly to himself. 'You reckon we should give him a hand, Halfneck?'

Quire took a step forward to the edge of the boardwalk and stared at the sight of Billy Jay anchored to his ankles in the mud. He aimed a long, arcing line of spittle into a pool of rainwater and watched the ripples shimmer. A sliver of mist swirled across his legs. 'Mebbe there's another way,' he muttered.

He rubbed his hands together, spat again, drew his Colt in a flash of fingers and fired a single shot that spun Billy Jay's gun from his hand.

The town men twitched. Sheriff Caulk stiffened. Cuts Bailey and Charlie Mint simply stared, open-mouthed. Ben McKellan stood protectively with his back to the store door. Pop Ryder bit deeper into the stem of his corncob.

'Nice shootin', friend,' grinned Drone. 'Now what? How about—'

Quire fired another four shots fast and at random into the mud round Billy's feet. Billy winced, ducked, almost lost his balance, tried to lift his legs, failed to move them an inch, and could only stand there, his gaze bewildered, glazed and wide, the sweat streaming down his mud-streaked face.

'I like it!' smiled Drone, drawing his own Colt as he repeated the flurry of shots into the mud at Billy's feet. 'Time you moved, boy,' he shouted above the roar of his gun. 'We go on like this the mud'll be flyin' like gnats on a green pond. Shift, damn you, shift!'

'Stop it! Stop it!' yelled Caulk, shouldering his way through the growing press of town men. 'Put them guns away. Put 'em away. Let's have no more—'

Quire swung round to face sheriff, his Colt levelled firm and steady in his grip. 'Not another step, mister, not if you want to see this day out.' He prodded the gun forward. 'This ain't none of your business. This is *our* business, Scoone business, and we'll settle it the Scoone way.'

'Not in my town you won't,' flared Caulk. 'Damned if you will! Now, do as I say and stop this, put them guns—'

Quire fired a single shot that ripped through Caulk's shirt, skimming across his shoulder like a red-hot branding iron. 'Next time it'll be plumb through your head,' scowled Quire.

Blood poured through Caulk's fingers as he gripped the wound and seethed his curses. Cuts Bailey and Charlie Mint stuffed bandannas under his shirt to staunch the flow.

'Anybody else wanna make a statement?' growled Quire waving his gun menacingly across the faces of the silent town men. His eyes pierced in the darkness of his glare. 'No? Then in that case my partner here will continue with his efforts to relieve the misery of the young fella stuck in the mud there.'

Keefer Drone twirled his Colt through his fingers. 'Only too happy to oblige, my friend,' he tittered, giving the Colt a final twirl above his head.

Billy Jay struggled desperately to pull his boots clear of the mud, to lift his legs, but could only writhe like a pinned insect, his arms swaying to hold his balance, his face smeared with a streaming mixture of sweat, splashed rainwater and thickening street dirt. He could only stare and dribble from the corner of his mouth as Drone's Colt descended from its twirling height and levelled like a condemning finger.

But Keefer Drone never pulled the trigger.

# CHAPTER THIRTEEN

The blaze and roar of the rifle shots filled the street like the onset of another wild storm. Lead splattered into the boardwalk, peppering the timbers at Drone's feet until the slivers were flying fast as maddened hornets. The gunslinger fell back, skipping and dancing clear of the hail of gunfire and splinters before crashing into Halfneck Quire to bring them both crashing to the boards in a twisted tangle of arms and legs. Billy Jay stood open-mouthed, staring, motionless in the grip of the street mud.

Lanky Joe rose carefully from behind the batwings and took in what he could see of the sudden mayhem. The crowd of town men had broken into smaller groups, some to bury themselves in doorways, behind the crates and barrels that always seemed to clutter the street by the store, others to dive into whatever cover they could find, wherever it was closest.

Sheriff Caulk found himself sharing the scant protection of a damaged crate with Pop Ryder.

'Who the hell's doin' the shootin'?' he croaked, ducking instinctively at another hail of shots that bit into the boardwalk fronting the Golden Gaze like steel teeth.

Pop's eyes were narrowed to dark slits as he swung his probing gaze across the rooftops and higher windows of the buildings facing the saloon. 'Darned if I can see. Mist ain't cleared yet, but whoever's doin' the shootin's gotta be doin' it from up there.... Hold it, what's that?' He risked pointing to the roof above Charlie Mint's saddlery. 'Ain't that...?'

'I saw it,' said Caulk. 'Could've been anybody. Or it might've been—'

'Hell, look you there,' groaned Pop.

All eyes in the smoke-filled, mist-grey street turned as the saloon batwings creaked open and Edrow Scoone stepped onto the boardwalk, his left arm round the neck of a young bar girl.

He glared at the sprawled tangle of Drone and Halfneck Quire. 'On your miserable feet, the pair of you, and get inside.' He waited until he had the boardwalk to himself, then stepped forward, dragging the girl across his body. 'If there's anybody here who figures shootin' me, go right ahead. You're goin' to have to blast through this pretty little body first. And that'd be a real shame.'

The groups of town men stayed silent. Would the unseen gunman risk a shot? Where was he now? *Who* was he, damn it?

'And as for the smart sonofabitch who's been doin' all the fancy shootin',' grinned Scoone, 'well, now, I got a message for him: Get out while you still got a chance, mister, 'cus you're sure as hell in for a painful time. I'm comin' to get you, fella, you bet I am. And when I lay my hands on you....' He spat. 'That's a pleasure I got comin'.'

The girl struggled for a moment against the grip across her throat. Scoone tightened his hold and called for Bullets Machin to join him. 'Get that fool youth out of that mud, then tie him up 'til I'm good and ready to hang the brat.' He spat again. 'You hear that, you town men – we're goin' to have a hangin'? Yessir! Right there in the livery corral where I hanged that blacksmith. And mebbe, as a special treat, we'll strip this tasty whore and string her up alongside him. How about that, eh?'

Scoone sneered. 'Mess with me at your peril!'

'The man ain't sane. He's mad. Ravin' mad.' Cuts Bailey swallowed, ran a bandanna round his neck and stretched out his hands to the warmth of the forge fire.

'Ain't no doubtin' to that,' agreed Charlie Mint, 'but it don't get us anywhere, does it? Scoone'll hang Billy Jay sure as drawin' breath, he will, and that gal along of him.'

'Not a gal?' said a town man, joining Cuts at the forge. 'Damn it, she's a female. You don't go hangin' females.'

'You do if you're Scoone,' clipped Charlie.

Pop Ryder leaned back in his seat in the open-fronted lean-to livery workshop and lit his pipe. 'Anybody checked on that stranger?' he asked, glancing over the cloud of smoke.

'What's there to check on?' asked Cuts. 'Nobody seems to have seen him, savin' mebbe Lanky Joe, but everybody seems to know he's here.'

'Well, it sure as hell weren't no angel of mercy firin' them shots this mornin'!' said Charlie. 'They were real. Real as you'll ever see. And whoever was firin' 'em knew exactly what he was doin' – and doin' it, I reckon, from my roof!'

'Mebbe we should try makin' contact with the fella,' mused a man sucking on a length of straw stalk. 'Could be he needs our help, assumin' he's stayin' around for some reason. Gotta be a reason, ain't there?'

Pop blew a slow eddy of smoke. 'He ain't here for his

health, that's for certain. But if Scoone's his reason for bein' here, then it can mean only one thing.'

'And what's that?' asked Cuts.

'He's been followin' the rat. Trailin' him. Sittin' close enough some place to watch his every move. And now he's mebbe figurin' he's got him penned.'

'Are you sayin' as how Scoone don't know to this?' said the man with the straw.

'Mebbe he does. Mebbe he don't.' Pop watched a smoke ring drift and spread on a shimmer of air. 'Either way, it looks like Random's goin' to be the place for the showdown. And we're all in the crossfire, ain't we? Every last man of us. . . .'

Lanky Joe gripped his besom in a tight, sticky grip and made his slow, solemn way through the saloon batwings to the boardwalk.

Never, in all his years of tending bar, serving folk, day in, night out, looking to the well-being of property, maintaining decent standards, keeping a place clean and tidy as befits a man who could not abide idleness or sloth – never had he seen anything like this. The state of his boardwalk – an area he had kept swept and spotless since the day he moved into the Golden Gaze as its sole proprietor – was beyond words, save those he mouthed under his breath and were not for general ears.

It was scarred, chipped, scraped, shot to pieces such as he might have only dreamed of in nightmares. Nothing, no amount of sweeping, scrubbing, brushing would ever restore it to its once pristine condition.

And it had all happened in minutes.

Minutes of madness. There was no other way of putting it. All that shooting, that flying lead. . . . Damn it, it was nothing short of a miracle that there was still a boardwalk left. And what would folk think now every time they stepped across it? What would *he* think every time he came to sweep it? He would think—

And then he would have to check himself. The shooting, the flying lead had saved the life for now of Billy Jay. If whoever had fired those shots – darned near emptied his Winchester into the timbers – had not been there. . . . Hell, had it been the stranger up there on the roof? It must have been him. There was no one else it could have been. So who was he; where was he now? Would he be back?

Lanky swished the besom across the battered boards. There were times when a fellow paid a high price to stay working.

He muttered darkly and swept on.

Doc Marchman rose silently from the side of the bed where Patsy Newbutt had slipped into a fitful doze, and tiptoed to the door of the room above the saloon.

All quiet now. The shooting was over. Scoone and his sidekicks would be mulling over matters aided by a bottle of Lanky's best. They had a deal to think about! But, damn it, would Scoone go ahead with his promise to hang Billy Jay with one of the bar girls along of him?

Doc listened carefully, his ear pressed to the door. No sound of voices. No one moving. He grunted softly, turned from the door and crossed to the window where the drapes were only part drawn.

He peered into the deserted street. The mist still hung like abandoned breath, but the rain had eased away for the time being. Now only streaks of heavy cloud blurred the once high skies. Bad weather was hanging on, thought

Doc. It was not done yet. There would be more rain, more swirling, clinging mists – and doubtless more blood to be washed away, more fear among the townfolk to be contained and calmed. And how many more Billy Jays were waiting in the shadows, filling their heads full of self-styled bravado, just itching to draw on any one of Scoone's men?

He grunted quietly again and turned sharply at the nervous tap on the door.

He greeted Alice with a quick smile and ushered her into the room. 'Well?' he asked, 'you see anythin'?'

'Nothin',' murmured the girl. 'I've been watchin' close on an hour, but he ain't showed. Mebbe it's like I said – I could've been mistaken. But somehow I don't figure so.'

'I'm glad you told me,' assured Doc. 'And I don't think you were mistaken. You saw somebody out there sure enough, and he's still here. We've just had a demonstration of that out there on the boardwalk! What we need to do now is keep a watch for the fella. We need his help, there's no doubtin' that, but mebbe he needs ours. We've gotta be there for him if he does. But, please don't ask me who the fella is or why he's here. I've not the slightest notion. I'm just grateful for the moment that he is.'

The girl hugged herself into the comfort of the shawl across her shoulders. 'Hope you're right, Doc, but meantime me and the girls are scared – real scared. You reckon Scoone'll do like he threatened? He goin' to hang Billy Jay and one of us?'

Doc sighed, glanced quickly at the still sleeping Patsy, and drew Alice to the far side of the room. 'I've gotta plan,' he began. 'Well, more of an idea really. It involves the girls. You wanna hear? But there ain't a lot of time. One of them scum will be checkin' on me before very long.'

'They're all drinkin' right now. We shan't be disturbed,' said Alice, her eyes brightening hopefully. 'Tell me what you've got in mind. Damn it, we gotta do somethin'. . . .'

# CHAPTER FOURTEEN

The morning dragged mournfully through to noon. The mist cleared to a grey backdrop against the still greyer, heavier clouds. Rain eased, gathered again, fell in a sudden torrent, then settled to a steady, persistent drizzle.

Sheriff Caulk watched it all from, first, his office, the boardwalk and finally from beneath the dripping over-hang at the livery forge.

'Set in for a long haul,' observed Pete Phillips, shaking the downpour from his patched long coat. 'Time of year, I guess,' he added absently. He hung the coat on a hook nearest the forge. 'I've just come from Bart Marsden's place, south end of the town.'

Caulk grunted as he cupped his hands to shield the match flame lighting his cigar. 'And?' he asked, raising his eyes from the glow.

'There's trouble brewin',' said Pete. 'Jake Shipman, Wes Splendow, Harry Green and a whole crowd of others are talkin' in Bart's barn.'

'What they sayin'?' murmured Caulk, tunnelling a line of smoke across the drizzle.

'They're sayin' as how they ain't much for doin nothin'

against Scoone and his scumbags. They figure Scoone'll go ahead and hang Billy Jay; probably a gal to follow. And that'll only be the start. Every time Scoone is crossed or somethin' don't suit, he'll kill another, then another 'til there ain't hardly nobody left. Women and little 'uns alike.' Pete paused to shift the coffee pot nearer the forge heat. 'Talk when I left was around the notion of stormin' the saloon. A dozen, fifteen men; guns blazin'; just shoot their way in and keep on shootin' 'til the rats are dead.'

The sheriff remained silent, thoughtful. He blew smoke, examined the tip of his cheroot, narrowed his eyes in a long gaze into the grey light and the steady drizzle. 'You reckon they'll do it?' he asked quietly.

'They're of a mind in their talk. But that ain't the doin', is it? They reckon it bad enough for Jed to die like he did – hanged like some common, two-bit hotshot – and then there's the Newbutts gettin' shot up out there at the homestead. And Patsy – what about her? Fella don't swallow what they did to her without it stickin' in the gullet. I tell you straight up, Mr Caulk, them town men are in an ugly mood. And, no disrespect, I don't figure they'll be the slightest bit inclined to give the law so much as the time of day when the bit bites. Their blood's up. It's survival or nothin'.'

Caulk waited again before speaking. 'You goin' to join 'em, Pete?'

'Have a mind to if I listen to my heart. But my head says other.' He shifted the coffee pot another careful inch. 'I'm thinkin' of the stranger we got in town. What's he doin', f'chris'sake? Has he got some sort of a score to settle with Scoone? Mebbe we should go find him; hear what he's got to say. After all, he saved Billy Jay's life back there,' he sighed. 'I don't know, Mr Caulk. Whole thing's one heaped up mess. But right now, it's lookin' an odds on certainty that Doc Marchman's goin' to be the busiest man in town.'

Sheriff Caulk blew smoke, watched the rain and wondered what the mist was hiding.

It was an hour after noon when Halfneck Quire and Keefer Drone left the Golden Gaze, crossed the street to Ben McKellan's store and began to help themselves from the well-stocked shelves.

'You fellas need some help there?' asked the proprietor, wearing his welcoming storekeeper's smile even though a soft beading of sweat had broken out on his brow. 'Fine selection of most things there. Some same as you'd find in them fancy stores back East. Yessir, we try to keep apace of things here in Random. You bet.' The smile flickered and weakened; the sweat gleamed.

Of the three customers already in the store, Miss Trudy Prufitt, trim and prim as ever in her full black dress with its high-neck lace collar, her black boots buffed to a deep shine, and her flowered bonnet set firm and pinned to reveal a carefully arranged show of grey curls, was the first to speak in her well-honed forthright manner: 'I hope you young fellas are stockin' up there in preparation for an imminent departure. Frankly, we've had enough of you. I'd personally like to see you brought to book for the behaviour you've displayed here in our town, but if that ain't goin' to come to pass, then be gone with you! There'll be somebody out there ready to deal with you sooner or later. Sooner as far as I'm concerned!'

Miss Prufitt stiffened and straightened to her full five feet two inches and tightened her two-handed grip on her wicker basket.

Shy Mrs Bates, hovering at Miss Prufitt's shoulder, her round eyes unblinking, her fingers twisting and turning among themselves, began to shiver. Old Zed Burben, clamped an empty pipe in his mouth, took a firm hold on his gnarled walking stick, and glared.

'Well, now, ain't no cause for. . . .' soothed the store-keeper, his words trailing away as Halfneck Quire turned, a pile of shirts in his arms, and stared at Miss Prufitt.

'You addressin' me there, ma'am?' he growled, easing the shirts to the counter.

'I most certainly am,' resumed Miss Prufitt. 'I have never seen, never, such a display of outright animal behav-iour in my so-called fellow human bein's. Have you no shame, no spark of decency in you? Your treatment of young Patsy Newbutt is nothin' short of diabolical. And as for what you did to her family, to Mr Chargers at the livery, the cold-blooded murder of Jessie Brown, and all that you've committed since you so unfortunately rode in here. . . . Well, really, have you thought what your mothers would say if they could see you now?'

Quire continued to stare in silence. Keefer Drone turned from the pile of pants he had been examining. Mrs Bates's eyes grew rounder and brighter. Zed Burben grunted his approval and agreement.

'I'm sure the lady don't mean—' began Ben McKellan again.

'I'm sure I mean every word of what I'm sayin', Mr McKellan,' continued Miss Prufitt defiantly. 'And I'll thank you not to put words into my mouth or attempt to pervert them. Stick to your storekeepin', sir! Now, as for you young varmints—'

'You want I should shoot her, Halfneck?' sneered Drone, dancing his fingers over the butt of his holstered Colt.

'Now hold on there,' began Ben again.

Mrs Bates gasped and shuddered. The old man thudded his stick to the floor.

Miss Prufitt pulled the basket tighter to her body. 'Shoot her – that appears to be your answer to everything, doesn't it? Well, if you so wish, then do it. Do it, right here, in full sight of these folk, just like you did to young Jessie Brown. But not before my friends here have finished their shopping.'

She indicated for Mrs Bates and Zed Burben to continue their browsing. Her glare settled on the sidekicks. 'And if you're plannin' on leavin' with them shirts and pants you're fingerin' there, be sure you pay for 'em. Cash.' She raised her head haughtily. 'I doubt if Mr McKellan will be givin' you credit.'

'Lippy old hag, ain't she?' grinned Drone. 'I've a mind to finish her here and now.'

'Gentlemen, gentlemen . . . Miss Prufitt . . . please, I beg of you, no trouble, not here in the store,' flustered McKellan, trying to place himself between Miss Prufitt and Keefer Drone. 'There's been enough—'

'Get her out,' ordered Quire. 'Out! Now! And if she ain't gone in ten seconds flat, I'll shoot the hag myself!'

Miss Prufitt fumed her anger, but offered no resistance as McKellan ushered her towards the door, Mrs Bates shivering and shaking in their wake, Zed Burben stamping and muttering behind them.

'You may think you own this town,' called Miss Prufitt over her shoulder, 'but believe me there's someone here who's watching you very closely. Very closely indeed. You've already had a taste of him. Oh, yes. But there's more to come. You mark my words. A whole sight more to come. . . .'

Ben McKellan closed the door on his customers, mopped the sweat from his brow and tried hard to summon a smile as he turned back to face Scoone's side-kicks.

'Now, how can I—?'

But that was as far as the storekeeper went. In the next moment three fast rifle shots had roared and blazed across the grey light shattering one of the store's two front windows. Halfneck Quire and Keefer Drone could only dive for cover behind their piles of selected shirts and pants on the polished counter.

# CHAPTER FIFTEEN

The once silent, rain-soaked street was suddenly alive and bristling as the rage of the gunfire whined and then echoed into the massed clouds above Random.

Sheriff Caulk and Pop Ryder were the first to appear on the boardwalk fronting the sheriff's office.

'Get into cover – now!' he yelled, directing Miss Prufitt, Mrs Bates and Zed Burben to retreat from the line of fire.

Cuts Bailey and Charlie Mint appeared as if from nowhere and guided the three stranded store customers to safety in the depths of Charlie's saddlery.

Lanky Joe pushed open the 'wings to the saloon and gazed into the street like a startled gopher. Two afternoon drinkers came to his side. Edrow Scoone and Bullets Machin watched from the safety of the shadows, the drift of the smoke from their freshly lit cigars being the only indication of their presence.

Doc Marchman showed his face briefly, anxiously at an upstairs window at the saloon, then let the drapes fall back again.

The men who had gathered at Bart Marsden's place in a meeting to discuss what might be done against Scoone, had reached the street within minutes and concentrated their gazes immediately on rooftops and first-floor windows.

'It's that darned stranger again,' murmured Jake Shipman, bringing his scan through a full half-circle left to right. 'He's up there, sure enough.'

'Who's in the store?' asked Harry Green.

'We'll be seein' any minute if they show their ugly faces again,' said Wes Spendlow.

'That fella, whoever he is, sure knows how to handle a rifle, I'll give him that,' muttered Bart, narrowing his eyes to dark slits.

'Hell, just look at McKellan's window,' hissed Harry. 'Ben ain't goin' to take one bit kindly to that.'

Sheriff Caulk, with Pop Ryder still at his side, had edged carefully through the darker reaches of the boardwalk towards the saloon, his gaze flicking constantly to the door of the store, his mind racing with the prospects of what might happen when it opened.

Gathering town men eased aside for him as he made his slow way onward, their voices – questions, speculations, wild observations – trailing after him like echoes:

'What's happenin', Sheriff?'

'We got a blood bath comin' up?'

'Them rats cornered?'

'God willin' let's pray so.'

'Is that right – Ben McKellan's dead?'

'Shot through the head, I hear.'

'They got women in there, Sheriff?'

'They'll rape 'em all – one by one.'

'Then shoot 'em.'

'Much more of this, and I'm pullin' out. I ain't stayin' to get shot.'

'He's got a point there. That's all we're doin' – waitin'

to get shot. . . .'

Caulk and Pop Ryder crossed quickly to the boardwalk at the Golden Gaze to be greeted with a nod and mournful roll of his eyes by Lanky Joe.

'Keefer Drone and Quire are in there,' said Lanky, conscious of Edrow Scoone pushing open the 'wings, a cloud of drifting cigar smoke proceeding him.

'I got two of my men in there, Sheriff,' he drawled, the smoke clouding from his mouth. 'So what you goin' to do about it? You're the law around here, I expect *my* sheriff to take care of *my* town. I ain't for havin' no smart-shootin' show offs on the premises. Get rid of the scum.'

Bullets Machin's fingers spread like weeds across the butt of his Colt.

Lanky Joe swallowed and buried his hands in the glass-cloth he was carrying. The afternoon drinkers stared in silence.

The town folk, watching from wherever they thought they might be safe – but with a clear view of everything that was happening – stood without murmur or movement.

Fisty Fox approached cautiously from the livery, indicating to Caulk that he would be there to watch the sheriff's back if he chose to cross from the saloon to the store.

Would he? Would he have the guts to bring Drone and Quire out of the store with his own gun trained on them? And what then? How long would it take for Scoone and Machin to let fly the lead from their own guns?

'And just so's you understand the situation,' continued Scoone, raising his voice to be heard the length of the street, 'if anythin' should happen to either one of my partners holed up in that goddamn store – anythin' at all – I'll put that mercantile to the torch *and* I'll hang another gal along of the one whose pretty little neck I'm already plannin' to stretch.'

He gazed round the drained, grey faces watching him. 'Do I make myself clear? I hope so. And especially to the sonofabitch who fancies himself with that Winchester but who ain't man enough to show his face to Edrow Scoone.'

A thicker cloud of smoke drifted from Scoone's mouth. 'Looks like it's over to you, Sheriff,' he grinned.

Sheriff Caulk gritted his teeth and suppressed a fuming desire to tell Edrow Scoone precisely what he thought of him, his miserable sidekicks and this whole nightmare of a situation his arrival in town had created.

Instead, he did his best with a look of disdain and turned to Pop Ryder.

'I'm goin' across there,' he said quietly. 'Don't let anybody follow me, and don't f'chris'sake start any shootin'.'

The silence stiffened like a board as Caulk stepped into the squelching street mud. He chose his steps carefully, deliberately, conscious of the eyes that were following his every move, some waiting for him to make a mistake, sink a boot into deeper mud, slip and lose his balance, or worse, fall flat on his back. The ooze and squelch of every footfall and heavy lift seemed to fill the street and drown even the silence.

He tightened his gaze on the store. One window had been completely shattered to leave a black staring space in which nothing moved and no sound drifted. Shards of broken glass littered the boardwalk like chipped ice. The door was closed, the place dead as if abandoned.

But somebody was watching, had to be.

Were Drone and Quire positioned either side of the

shattered window? Were they holding Ben McKellan hostage against another burst of rifle shots from the rooftops? Did they intend bringing him out as a shield to their escape? What did they plan now that the law was closing in? Or were they the law?

The questions raged through the sheriff's head until he thought it would burst. But he held to his steady steps. Now he was a touch over halfway across the street. The silence had thickened. The probing, watchful stares intensified. He felt like a man in quicksand with an audience content only to watch.

He slowed. It was time to make a decision. Did he step clear of the street, approach the door of the store, then call for the sidekicks to come out, bringing McKellan with them? Or did he halt where he stood, sinking ever deeper into mud?

He cursed under his breath, gathered his inner strength and pushed on, but had taken no more than a single step, when all hell broke loose.

It was the voice that halted him and forced him to squelch round to face the way he had come.

'Up there,' shouted a town man from somewhere in the depths of a boardwalk. 'Up there – the fella with the rifle! He's there, right now!'

The man had pushed his way to the front of the throng of folk to point to the span of roof across the Golden Gaze, and was gesturing wildly still shouting, as all eyes followed his raised arm.

It was him, sure enough, thought Caulk. It was the stranger. No mistake. But what in the name of—?

The sheriff fought for his balance at the sudden crack and blaze of Bullets Machin's Colt as the sidekick plunged from Scoone's side on the boardwalk and fired what seemed like an almost loose shot towards the saloon roof.

Caulk's throat felt suddenly pinched between dry rocks as he watched the dark, silhouetted shape of the stranger falter in what he must have intended to be his retreat from the rooftop, stand static for a moment, one hand flattening on his right shoulder, then begin a slow, twisting plunge to the street.

No one moved. No one made a sound or mouthed so much as a gasp let alone a word; they could only watch until the body thudded to the ground in the alley flanking the saloon.

Caulk glanced hurriedly at the store where the door remained closed and the black eye of the shattered window as empty as night.

'Nice shootin' there, Bullets!' beamed Scoone, clamping his cigar between his teeth. A stream of smoke seeped through his stained teeth. 'Yeah ... real nice shootin'. And you know somethin', my friend, I do believe you may have got rid of that smart-shootin' sonofabitch who's been like a plague since we rode in here. Yeah ... I do believe you have.' He turned to Sheriff Caulk still standing in the street mud. 'You'd better be takin' a look at this, Sheriff.'

Caulk struggled free of the mud as the door to the store opened and Keefer Drone and Halfneck Quire stepped into the grim afternoon light.

# CHAPTER SIXTEEN

'He ain't dead. I know he ain't. I seen him twitch.' A town man sporting a crushed, battered derby gathered a crowd to him at the far end of the alley alongside the saloon. 'I'm tellin' you the truth here,' he insisted. 'I seen the fella soon as Doc got to him. He was bleedin' bad, but he weren't dead.'

A tall man wiped a hand over his grubby face and fixed his gaze on the saloon. 'They've got him in there now – Scoone, them rats of his, Doc and the sheriff.' The man swallowed tightly. 'You reckon Scoone'll finish him off?'

'He ain't goin' to let the fella live, that's for sure,' said an older man in a tone of grey resignation. 'Done too much damage already, ain't he? Too much of a threat.'

The group of men fell silent, their eyes fixed on the saloon as if reliving in their minds the moment of Machin's wild shot; the way the man on the roof had halted, hesitated, maybe grimaced under the pain of the shot, and then fallen – so slowly, it seemed, so deliberately, like a dark, dead bird, dropping – hit the ground and not moved.

'The sonofabitch got lucky with that shot,' murmured a man at the back of the group. 'Just lucky.'

'Must've heard somethin', seen somethin'. . . .' began another.

'It was the fella who yelled out. He did it,' said the man in the crushed derby. 'If he'd kept his mouth shut. . . . Why'd he have to go callin' out like that?'

The men lapsed to silence again. Someone lit a cheroot and blew smoke into the first mists of a slow drizzle. The tall man pulled the collar of his coat into his neck and buried his hands in his pockets. A thin man still in shirt-sleeves shivered. The fellow at his side spat into the mud.

'T'ain't no use blamin' folk,' said Charlie Mint, wiping a bandanna around his neck. 'Might just as well say it's all Miss Prufitt's fault for bein' in McKellan's store. If she hadn't spoke her mind like Ben says she did. . . .' He pocketed the bandanna. 'What the hell. It's done now, ain't it? Done and can't be undone. Fact is, we've lost the stranger – whoever he is.'

'Damn it, the fella was on our side. He was fightin' for us,' groaned the tall man. 'Best hope we had.'

The men murmured their agreement before falling back to their silence and staring.

'So what now?' asked one at last. 'What we goin' to do?'

The air in the Golden Gaze had thickened in a haze of cigar smoke, liquor and tense bodies; the light dimmed under the gathering of cloud and the low glow of the lanterns.

One corner of the saloon – with a clear view of the batwings – was occupied by Scoone and his sidekicks, their table already cluttered with empty bottles and stained glasses. Edrow Scoone sat alone, his gaze fixed on his glass as he turned it slowly through his fingers, each movement reflecting some measure of his thinking: in one turn decisive, in another still reckoning, perhaps unsure. From time to time his eyes lifted from the glass to focus on the man being tended by Doc Marchman, watched over by Sheriff Caulk.

'You know this man?' asked Caulk, as Halfneck Quire crossed the bar to take a closer look.

'I know him,' said Quire. 'You bet I do. We all do. Been sittin' on our butts these past three years. Must be somethin' personal to stay that close for that long.' He sneered. 'His name's Wilson. Marshal Henry Wilson. Hails from somewhere out Kansas way.'

'A lawman,' murmured Caulk, thoughtfully. 'Can't say I've crossed him before.'

'Well, don't go reckonin' on makin' a friend of him,' grinned Quire. 'He ain't goin' to be around long enough! We'll hang him along of that kid and one of the gals.'

'That'll be cold-blooded murder,' said Doc, rolling his shirtsleeves down to their cuffs. 'Damnit, the fella's hit pretty bad as it is. See for yourself. I'll do my best, but there's lead buried deep there. If I don't get to cuttin' it out soon. . . . Well, fact is, he may not make it.'

'He's a dead man any which way you see it,' smiled Drone, spinning his Colt through a whirl of fingers. 'I ain't fussed. I've seen enough of the fella. He gets on my nerves. Sooner he's dead the better.'

Scoone pushed back his chair, came to his feet and stared at the man. 'He'll die when I say. Soon as he comes round I wanna speak with him, so you just make sure he lives long enough, eh, Doc? And meantime, don't forget the little lady upstairs. I want her in one livin' piece. You understand?'

Doc closed his medicine bag with a sharp click, reached for his jacket and accepted the sheriff's help to slip into it.

'I'm in need of fresh bandages and medicines,' he said flatly. 'I need to go home.'

'Make it fast,' snapped Scoone. 'Bullets here will go with you.'

'I'm perfectly capable—' began Doc.

'You heard me, Doc. Bullets goes with you. So shift!' Scoone's black gaze settled on Caulk. 'And you, Sheriff, had best go get that street cleared of gawpin' folk. I'll give 'em somethin' to gawp at later!'

Sheriff Caulk stiffened. 'Well, before I get to organizin' *my* town the way *I* want,' he clipped tautly, 'you'd better get to figurin' recompense for Ben McKellan's store window. Somebody's goin' to have to pay.'

'Sure,' quipped Scoone, 'mention it to Marshal Wilson there when he comes round. I'm sure he'll be glad to oblige!'


'He's a marshal. He's the law. Didn't I say he was somethin' special? Knew it from the start.' Charlie Mint tapped a knowing finger across the side of his nose. 'Things are lookin' up, I'd say.'

'Well, I wouldn't,' said the town man in the straw hat, glancing furtively through the evening gloom to where a handful of low-lit lanterns illuminated the boardwalk. 'Lawman he may be, but he ain't a sight of use at the moment, is he, not shot up like Doc says he is and sittin' right there in Scoone's clutches? No use to us there, is he? Fact is, it's my bettin' one of them rats'll finish him before the night's out, and that'll be that.'

Charlie, Cuts Bailey, Pop Ryder and the group of town men huddled instinctively into the gathering darkness with a look of helpless resignation and foreboding on their faces, stares fixed on the brighter light in the Golden Gaze.

Pop lit his pipe. A town man scratched his neck. Cuts Bailey swayed gently to and fro, as if moving to the rhythm of his thoughts. Charlie consulted his timepiece, held it to the brighter light, grunted and pocketed it again with a flourish. He said nothing.

'Wilson . . . Wilson,' mused Pop, his eyes squinting against a sudden swirl of smoke from his pipe. 'I once heard of a Wilson time I was out ridin' herd along the bluegrass country. He was a lawman. Had quite a reputation.'

'Did he have a scar the length of his cheek?' asked Charlie.

'Don't know,' said Pop. 'Never met the fella. Just heard tell of him.'

The men fell silent again.

'When's Scoone goin' to make a move, f'chris'sake?' said a short, tubby man, his eyes blinking and twinkling behind wire framed spectacles.

'He goin' to sit suppin' and fandanglin' with them gals all night?'

'Don't know about Scoone movin', but somebody sure as hell is,' said Cuts.

The men turned as one at the sound of footsteps approaching through the gloom and misty drizzle.

'Oh, no,' murmured Charlie, 'not that. Not Bart Marsden and that bunch of his. . . .'

Bodies darkened and thickened in their approach along the boardwalk. Footfalls deepened, slowed and finally halted.

'What's this, Bart?' smiled Charlie almost light-heartedly. 'You headin' up some sort of deputation or somethin'? Goin' the wrong way if it's the sheriff you're lookin' for. He's in his office.'

Marsden's glance took in the town men, then settled to a steady, threatening glare on the glow at the Golden Gaze. 'We ain't interested in the sheriff,' he quipped, the edge to his voice verging on anger. 'Don't seem there's much he can do, anyhow. We're goin' about things our way. M'self, Wes here, Harry and the others, we figure the time's come to do somethin' positive.'

'It'll be positive all right, judgin' by them guns you're carryin',' said Pop, billowing a stream of pipe smoke across the drizzle. 'More like a body count, if you ask me.'

'We ain't,' snapped Wes Spendlow, taking a firmer grip of his Winchester. 'We're just plain gut-filled with the way things are goin'. Town ain't our own. There's goin' to be more shootin', more killin', hangin' and takin' our women. . . . Lord knows where it's goin' or where it'll end. Somebody's got to stop it.'

Harry Green lifted and settled his hat nervously at Spendlow's shoulder. 'He's right. We gotta make a move, 'specially now that stranger's been taken, and him a lawman at that. Damnit, he should've said somethin'.'

Charlie Mint's gaze narrowed on Marsden's face. 'So what exactly are you plannin' on doin'?'

'We're goin' to face up to Scoone. Tell him face-to-face that we ain't goin' on like this no more and if he don't get out, if he's set on defyin' us, well, he'll know the consquences. There'll be no quarter given. We shan't be for jailin' 'em, it'll be out-and-out shootin' 'til there ain't one of 'em standin'. And if some of us pay with our lives, so be it. We're willin' enough.'

The mood among the men was tense and totally silent for a long half minute.

'All very noble of you, Bart,' said Pop at last, studying the glow of ash in the bowl of his pipe. 'Very noble. You and the fellas there are to be admired for standin' to your principles. Sure, you should . . . And then pitied for the fools you are!'

Marsden gritted his teeth angrily. Wes Spendlow lifted the Winchester across his body. Harry Green fidgeted with his hat.

'And what do you know, old-timer?' mocked one of Marsden's men. 'I don't see you tellin' Scoone to shift his butt out of town.' His partners nodded and murmured their agreement. 'In fact, I don't see any of you doin' a darn thing. And that goes for our sheriff—'

'Now hold on there, fella,' urged Charlie. 'This ain't no time to go criticizin' Sheriff Caulk. Damnit, him and Doc—'

'How long before Scoone gets to hangin' Billy Jay?' growled Marsden. 'An hour . . . two? Midnight? Or mebbe keep the poor devil waitin' 'til tomorrow. And that lawman, Wilson; you don't reckon for Scoone lettin' him live, do you?' Marsden's glare came alight. 'And I'll tell you somethin' else,' he went on, warming to his outburst. 'It's only a matter of time before them rats tire of Lanky Joe's bar gals, and they grab that Patsy Newbutt again. And then mebbe they'll turn their rat-bag attention on the town women. My wife, Harry's wife.'

'My daughter,' piped Wes Spendlow.

'His daughter,' echoed Marsden. 'And a dozen more besides. Well, I ain't waitin' for that sort of hell. You bet I ain't. Nossir. So if you'll just stand aside there Charlie Mint, we'll be about our business.' Marsden took a step forward, then hesitated. 'Oh, and if you've a mind to go warnin' the sheriff of our intent, you go ahead. He'd mebbe like to come and give us a hand. Same goes for any of you fellas here.'

Charlie, Pop Ryder, Cuts Bailey and the others stood aside to let Marsen and his followers make their slow but determined way to the glow of the Golden Gaze.

'Like moths to a flame,' murmured Pop.

# CHAPTER
# SEVENTEEN

Lanky Joe's besom swept quietly through a sliver of dust and progressed rhythmically on its way through the dimly lit, smoke-hazed saloon.

But Lanky had only half his mind on dust; he was a whole sight more concerned with, firstly, the fellow in the corner – the one-time stranger who appeared now to be no less than a full-fledged lawman – and, second, young Billy Jay bound and gagged there to a chair in the darkest corner of the bar, awaiting what could only be described as his execution.

The lawman, the mysterious Henry Wilson, seemed to Lanky to be making good progress under Doc Marchman's concentrated attention. In fact, Doc had announced with a grunt of sheer triumph the removal of the lead from the man's shoulder only minutes ago.

'He's goin' to know to the pain for a time, but he'll be fine,' he had beamed, as if having resurrected the man from the very brink of death.

Well, maybe he had, thought Lanky, swishing on absent-mindedly. Not that it was going to do Marshal Wilson one bit of good. Scoone would shoot him, anyhow. Still, while there was life, there was always hope.

Meantime, Scoone and his sidekicks seemed in no great hurry to do anything or be anywhere other than here, drinking, eating, dozing, drinking some more and helping themselves to a girl whenever the mood took them. It was like living in a barrel of fetid water: the murk got thicker, the smell a whole lot worse, and the outlook bleaker by the hour. Unless something happened soon. . . .

And then, of course, it did.

'Hey, Scoone, give your butt an airin' and get yourself out here.'

There was no mistaking Bart Marsden's thick, gravel voice, or the uncharacteristic arrogance of its tone. Hell, thought Lanky, edging his way nearer the batwings, had Bart been drinking? Well, not here, that was for sure!

Scoone remained seated at his usual corner table. He said nothing, made no movement save to flick a quick glance at Bullets Machin as if giving an unspoken order.

Machin slid away to the right-hand side of the 'wings, Keefer Drone to the left. Halfneck Quire strode quickly but silently across the bar to the stairs and disappeared up them to the balcony above the saloon.

Lanky heard a door open, a girl stifle a gasp, the door close, then silence.

He swallowed and tightened his grip on the besom.

Doc Marchman turned his attention from his patient for a moment, glanced at Scoone, the sidekicks, then Lanky, before settling his steady gaze on the darkness beyond the 'wings. What now, he wondered?

Billy Jay squirmed helplessly in the chair in the shadows, gave up and simply stared, wide-eyed, pale and scared through to the pit of his rumbling gut.

'You hearin' me there?' called Marsden again. 'You'd

better be if you know what's good for you. Me and my fellow townsmen here have got somethin' to say. And we ain't for bein' messed with. Not this time. Not no way. So you get yourself out here right now. You hear me?'

Still Scoone remained seated. He glanced again at Machin, then at Drone; seemed to Lanky to mouth something; fell silent again and continued to turn an empty whiskey glass through his stained, calloused fingers.

'Mr Scoone's busy right now,' shouted Machin from the 'wings. 'You wanna make an appointment to see him, he'll state a convenient time.'

There was a low, barely audible murmuring among the town men gathered in the street. Lanky's fingers sweated on the handle of the besom. Doc felt an icy chill across the back of his neck. He was almost certain Marshal Wilson opened one eye for just a few flickering seconds, but when he looked closer the man was sleeping. Billy Jay had not so much as blinked.

Marsden's gravel voice spilled out again. 'We ain't for bein' treated like dirt. This is our town and we run it our way. Now if Scoone ain't got the decency to step out here and hear us, we'll just march right in there of our own accord. Choice is his. We'll give him two minutes. You hear . . . two minutes.'

Trouble . . . it was coming faster than a north wind bringing snow, thought Lanky. He could smell it. He eased aside from the direct line of fire from the street. No one seemed to notice. Where, he wondered, was Sheriff Caulk?

Billy Jay began to squirm again. Damn it, were they just going to leave him here? Sweat beaded and trickled from his brow. His throat was parched. Every muscle in his body ached and throbbed to a point where he thought they would burst. And now his sight was blurring. Shapes appeared, only to melt before him. Images crowded where images were not supposed to be. Maybe he would be better off dead.

'One more minute, Scoone, that's all you've got,' announced Marsden.

Scoone's gaze lifted from the whiskey glass. He glanced quickly at the clock behind the bar, nodded to Machin and Drone and came lazily to his feet as if about to undertake an annoying chore.

'If there's goin' to be lead flyin' here, I got a right to move my patient out of the line of fire,' piped Doc, a new note of authority in his voice.

Scoone hesitated, stared at Doc for a moment. 'Back of the bar,' he grunted. 'And make it quick.'

Doc gestured to Lanky to give him a hand. 'Keep your head down,' he murmured as the two struggled to ease the limp, seemingly lifeless body of the wounded marshal into the shadows at the rear of the saloon. 'This place is goin' to be a hell-hole in no time at all. Don't you goin' addin' to my work, you hear?' He patted Lanky on the shoulder and turned his attention back to the marshal.

Marsden's voice boomed again from the street. 'Time's up, Scoone. If you ain't comin' out, we're comin' in.'

Some reckoned later that Bart Marsden took no more than two steps before he was gunned down and fell to the street mud without so much as a twitch. Others say he reached the steps to the boardwalk fronting the Golden Gaze before he fell. And there were those who claimed he died in a hail of gunfire without moving.

It made little difference.

Bart Marsden lay dead within seconds of threatening to advance on Scoone. Harry Green, flanking his left, died as the result of three rapid shots from a first-floor bedroom window.

Wes Spendlow, advancing quickly from Marsden's right, led three town men in a direct assault on the saloon and was within feet of the 'wings when he took a direct burst of fire in the face and was flung back through a shower of his own blood. The men he was leading never laid a hand on the 'wings and fell, one atop the other, in a wet pile on the boardwalk.

The street erupted in the blown sheets of steady rain.

Sheriff Caulk, with Fisty Fox and Joe Dimes in his wake, shouted for the town men to halt, stay where they were. 'No good's goin' to come of this. You're only goin' to make things. . . .'

But his words and voice were drowned in the surge of the remainder of Marsden's followers in a sudden charge on the saloon. They growled, yelled, cursed and spat their anger, their sole desire to face Scoone and his men and kill them – and, in this mood, any other body that crossed them.

Gunfire filled the night, the town men firing wildly, without aim or target, and without a care so long as the shot blazed in the direction of the light in the saloon.

The retaliation left no one in doubt. Keefer Drone felled two men in almost as many seconds – and whooped his delight as a third squelched into range. Bullets Machin blew a man clean off the boardwalk and halfway across the street with a single shot from his long barrelled Colt, and watched him breathe his last face down in the mud. Halfneck Quire loosed lead at random from the upstairs window, spraying the street at will and wherever he saw a moving body. The bar girl pressed tight to the door at his back could only stare, too scared even to mouth a scream.

Inside the saloon, Lanky Joe had retreated to what he had figured would be safety among his bottles, boxes, glasses and cloths.

The move had been a big mistake.

Within minutes he was being showered by shards of broken glass, dripping liquids, splinters of timber, and deafened as the guns roared round him, the crash, crack, blaze and whine of every shot merging in a thickening chaos of sound until he thought his head would burst.

He could see nothing of Doc. Calling him had been lost in the mayhem. As far as Lanky knew, he might have caught a stray bullet and be bleeding to death somewhere, anywhere in the rubbish, dirt, dust and blood of what had once been his pride and joy. The cleanest saloon this side of the big divide.

He reached out instinctively. Where the hell was that besom. . . .

Back in the street, Sheriff Caulk was trying for the twentieth time to bring some sort of order to the deepening chaos.

'It's no good, boss,' coughed Fisty Fox, staggering to Caulk's side. 'They ain't listenin'. And now there's more of 'em joinin' in. It's like a fever.'

Caulk wiped sweat and dirt from his face and narrowed his gaze on the crowded street, the steady rain and the deepening mud. He wanted to shut his ears to the sound.

'They'll get nowhere while ever Scoone and his men are holed up in the saloon,' he shouted above the din. 'Every time they set a foot in the direction of the 'wings the lead flies. How many dead?'

'Lost count after a dozen,' groaned Fisty.

Caulk gritted his teeth and steadied his grip on his Winchester. 'That's enough,' he said. 'I'm goin' in. I'll try the back door if it's still unlocked. If not. . . . Do the best you can here – but for God's sake stay alive!'

He disappeared like a shadow into the rain-drenched night.

*

# CHAPTER EIGHTEEN

Caulk had stumbled no more than a dozen yards through the mud, the swirling rain and mêlée of bodies – some stunned and immobile, some angry and threatening, some dead – when Ben McKellan laid an anxious hand on his arm and gripped it.

'Town's fallin' apart,' he said, his rain-washed face glistening in the scrawl of lantern light. 'They're destroyin' it! Their own town, f'chris'sake! What we goin' to do? Damnit, what *can* we do?'

'Keep as many clear of the saloon as we can for a start. They're rushin' to their deaths minute they get near it. Scoone and his guns will keep blazin' for as long as the fools keep comin'. Like shootin' rats in a barrel.' Caulk tipped water from the brim of his hat. 'I'm goin' to try to get in.'

'On your own?' frowned Ben.

'If I can find a way through that back door. . . . We could mebbe get others in there. Just one of Scoone's men dead would make a difference.'

'I'm comin' with you,' insisted Ben. 'And no arguin'. We ain't doin' no good here. Let's move!'

The two men plunged away from the madness of the main street towards the pitch-black alley that ran alongside the bulk of the saloon. Once into it and free of the clamouring bodies intent on storming the bar they were able to move at a faster, more assured pace, threading their way through the flotsam of crates, barrels and boxes.

Ben cracked his shin against an upturned barrel, hissed a stream of curses and rolled it aside. A scared, stray dog slunk away, wimpering, tail between its legs, sniffing out a place of safety in the discarded crates.

Caulk was ahead now but beginning to slow the pace as the rear of the saloon came into view and took shape against the backdrop of swirling rain. The noise from the street rose to a new pitch. Men shouted and cursed; somebody groaned miserably, guns roared, a door splintered, windows smashed.

'See anythin'?' said Ben, crouching at the sheriff's side behind a broken crate. 'Anybody about?'

'Seems like they're all concentrated at the front,' murmured Caulk. He lifted his narrowed gaze to the small square windows of the rooms on the first floor. 'Quiet enough up there. The girls are stayin' low.'

'It's that rat Quire at the front who's doin' the damage. If we could get to him. . . .'

'Mebbe we can,' said Caulk. 'Let's get to that door – and keep our fingers crossed Lanky ain't locked it.'

They moved on, slinking through the dark like alley cats, sweat beading on their faces, their eyes fixed now on the single door to the rear of the saloon. Once in there, Caulk figured, he could maybe work a way up the shadowy stairs to the room where Quire was dousing the street with lead.

'What the hell's that?' hissed Ben at Caulk's side. He pointed to the night sky, or what there was of it in the drift of rain and sullen weight of black cloud. A part of it immediately above the street had lit up as if on fire.

'Torches,' croaked Caulk, swallowing on his parched throat. 'They've lit torches.'

Ben groaned. 'Hell, I just hope they know what they're doin', f'chris'sake. One stray spark and. . . .' He gulped. 'Mebbe the rain'll get heavier.'

'Come on,' urged Caulk.

Again they moved, this time more to the left of the door and out of the direct line of vision should it open and release a sudden splash of light. Not that Caulk reckoned it likely. All the action, the shooting, shouting, slipping and sliding through mud in the general mayhem, was still concentrated in the street and the frontage of the Golden Gaze. Nobody as yet had figured a need for the back door. Caulk muttered the 'as yet' under his breath, reached a clutter of empty barrels, crouched behind them and waited for Ben to join him.

'I'll go on alone from here,' he said softly. 'Cover me. Minute I have the door open you follow. Not before. You got it?'

Ben nodded. 'Go easy,' he whispered. 'Ain't no sayin' to what's on the other side.'

Caulk grunted, tapped the storekeeper on the shoulder, took stock of what he could make out of his surroundings and crept away without a sound.

Ben watched him, feeling his every step, every shift of his body as Caulk came nearer to the door. Surely, he thought, if there was anybody behind it, he would have made a noise by now.

But what would anyone be doing there? Scoone, Bullets Machin and Keefer Drone were all shooting from the saloon. Halfneck Quire was in a room overlooking the street. No saying as to Lanky Joe, Doc Marchman, the wounded marshal and young Billy Jay, not to mention Patsy and the bar girls. Maybe Scoone had shot them before the town men attacked. Maybe they had died in the crossfire.

Caulk was closer now. Almost there.

Ben wiped a cold, salty mixture of sweat and rain from his face, winced at the clinging chill and dampness of his clothes. Damn it, first thing he was going to do once this madness was over and daybreak and some warm sun were here, was go have himself a whole dollar's worth of Cuts Bailey's hot tub, and maybe treat himself at the same time to—

The backdoor to the saloon was flung open with a suddenness that made Ben McKellan's eyes pop almost clean out of their sockets.

Marshal Wilson!

What in the name of. . . ? Ben rose from his cover without a thought for what exposing himself might attract. He saw Sheriff Caulk come to his full height, his Winchester flat and loose across his body, and, like himself, simply stare as the lawman staggered for a moment, stumbled, found his balance, took in the chill night air and the drizzling rain, then slid away to the darkness as if swallowed by it.

The last Ben saw of him before he became a part of the night was the flash of the white bandage across his shoulder.

Ben shifted like a startled rat through the backdoor flotsam to Caulk's side. Both men dropped to one knee behind a sodden crate.

'Tell me I ain't seein' things, f'chris'sake,' hissed Ben. 'That who I think it was – right? I ain't dreamin'?'

'No, you're not,' said Caulk, ducking lower instinctively at the roar and blaze of another round of gunfire. 'But how come. . . ? And just where . . . where in hell is Doc? Just what's goin' on in there?'

Both men settled their gaze on the door as it swung loosely in the night wind for a moment before closing with a slow click as if an invisible hand had drawn it back to its place.

'You figure for that lawman makin' a run for it?' asked Ben.

'I ain't got a clue what's happenin' and that's the truth of it. Whole town's gone mad.'

More shots whined and echoed into emptiness. Another window smashed under what sounded like a body crashing through it. The rain squalled. The night wind seemed to groan.

Ben gulped. 'Fella ain't goin' to get far with that wounded shoulder, that's for sure. Couldn't handle a soft rein never mind a gun.' He squinted across the darkness. 'Mebbe we should go after him. Mebbe he saw us. God, if he did, why the hell didn't he say somethin'?' He wiped rain from his face again. 'He'll be lucky to make it across the street.'

'He'll have to take his chance same as the others,' said Caulk. 'I've got the folk holed up in the saloon to reckon to.'

'We goin' in?'

'You bet. Cover me again. Soon as I get—'

'Oh, my God,' moaned Ben. 'Just look at that.'


Swirling, licking tongues of flame were reaching into the darkness above the street with an intensity that blinded.

Caulk and Ben raised hands to shield their eyes against

the glaring brightness that spread and filled the sky with a searing glow. It seemed to Ben that the doors to a giant forge had been flung open in a fit of madness.

The gunfire ceased. Voices fell silent. Flames roared and crackled. Sparks soared high and wide like crazed fireflies. Horses at the livery snorted and neighed their panic; a door banged on the wind as it whipped the flames into still fiercer, hotter swirls that threatened to reduce Random to a pile of mourning ash.

# CHAPTER NINETEEN

The fire raged for another half-hour. Cuts Bailey's barbering premises were gutted to a mass of charred timber and ash. Three-quarters of Charlie Mint's saddlery was lost to the flames. Miraculously, much of McKellan's store escaped the worst, while store sheds, old barns, shacks, the timber yard simply disappeared as standing structures. The spaces left were no more than swamps of black ash and mud. And when at last the drizzling rain broke to a steady downpour that finally doused the flames, the street began to steam.

'Last breath of the dead,' had been one murmured opinion.

No one knew or cared to say how the blaze began: a loose shot; a mishandled torch; a deliberate act of arson. The possibilities seemed as endless as the night itself.

But the miracle had been, as Pop Ryder was quick to point out, that the shooting had stopped and not a single soul had been lost to the flames.

'That may be so, Pop,' an exhausted town man had offered as he joined the group in the scant cover of a half-burned barn, 'but them rats are still there, aren't they? Still in the saloon. And they're still holdin' our town – what there is of it. Damn it, at this rate, there ain't goin' to

112

be nothin' nor nobody left!'

'Mebbe we should've let the flames do their worst,' a second man had quipped, expressing an opinion that had found ready support.

'We've lost good men tonight and darn near a half the town. What next? Can it get any worse?'

'More deaths, more fire? Mebbe we're creatin' our own Hell right here in Random.'

'Mebbe this *is* Hell. Mebbe it always was.'

'That's fool talk and you know it. Damnit, we had a decent livin' here. Now look at us. Listen to us. We're talkin' like it's all over.'

'Back where we started, that's for sure. And men have died for it. Men whose sweat helped build this town – Wes Spendlow, Bart Marsden, Harry Green, a dozen others. Died for nothin', every last one of 'em.'

'How we goin' to bury them decent and still sleep at nights?'

'Well, I'm of a mind to get myself back there. Go hit that saloon for all it's worth; every last bullet I've got with every last breath in my body. That's what I'm for. Who's with me?'

A half-dozen men had stepped forward in support of the opinion when Sheriff Caulk appeared through the gloom, half shadows and smoke and glared at the men like an angry hawk.

'Nobody's with you,' he snapped. 'Nobody, you hear, not if they've got any sense.'

'All very well sayin' that, Sheriff, but—'

'But nothin'.' Caulk wiped a filthy hand over his already filthy face, spreading the dirt so that his eyes shone through it like lights. 'Damnit, you've only got to look round you. What have we got? What's left? Very little.

We've got bodies to collect and bury; a town to start clearin' so that the livin' can go on doin' just that. There's women and young ones to look to.' His eyes widened. 'This town ain't done, not by a long shot. What we don't need is more dead bodies. We need the livin'.'

'And them back there – them folk still in the saloon – what we goin' to do about them? Leave 'em? Forget 'em? We turnin' our backs on them, Sheriff?'

'The hell we are,' snapped Caulk again. 'I'm dealin' with that situation.'

'Not by yourself, you ain't,' clipped a town man.

'Well, mebbe I ain't alone,' said Caulk, staring into the drifting smoke. 'The lawman got clear in the chaos. Wilson's out there somewhere.'

The town men fell to a watchful silence.


Edrow Scoone aimed a line of spittle over the batwings to the mud and blood-caked boardwalk fronting the Golden Gaze and stared at the charred, blackened skeletons of the buildings opposite. His luck had held, he mused. The fire had burned itself out and died in the downpour before having a chance to reach across the street.

He watched, his eyes narrowing, saliva thickening at the corner of his mouth, as two men carted a dead body out of sight. He smiled thinly. A dozen, fifteen . . . he had lost count of how many had died that night. It hardly mattered by his reckoning.

But now, he knew, the town was his. It would take days for the dead to be collected and buried, then maybe weeks to begin rebuilding the street and for folk to settle again. And meantime, he would be here, watching every move, consolidating his hold, appreciating his retirement, the easy days of comfort, just as he had always planned.

But there was still Wilson.

Not killing the marshal when the chance had been there was a big mistake. Allowing the fellow to slip away in the mayhem of the shooting, the darkness in the saloon when a lantern had shattered, had only honed the mistake. Now it cut at him even though he knew the lawman to be wounded and probably unable to handle a gun with any accuracy.

But you never underestimated Wilson, not if you valued seeing another sun come up. Scoone knew that well enough. He had lived through three long years of having the fellow as close as a second shadow to learn it, feel it, see and hear it. And now he was here again, just like a bad smell you could never escape. Damn it, the fellow was a haunting.

'Me and Bullets here are for doin' what we should've done long back,' said Keefer Drone, sauntering to Scoone's side. 'We're goin' out there to find Wilson just as soon as it's first light. Get the business over with; that sonofabitch lawman off our backs once and for all. Should've done it years back.'

'You had your chances as I recall,' sneered Scoone. 'That time back at Long Rocks, you had him plumb in your sights. How come you missed?'

'Wilson got lucky, same as he always does, same as he did here tonight,' clipped Drone with a sharp, resentful glance at Scoone. 'That doc should've kept a grip on the fella. He's mebbe lyin' about how bad the rat is wounded. Mebbe he's workin' along of him; helpin' him. What say we drag him away from that gal he's supposed to be tendin' upstairs. Let's hear what he's got to say. I'll get him talkin' sure enough. Just watch me!'

'Leave him,' ordered Scoone. 'We need a doc. Place

ain't settled proper without a doc.'

Drone sniffed and circled the tip of his boot across the floor. 'We've been talkin' about that – me and Bullets.'

'You and Bullets seem to have real long tongues these days. So what you been discussin', or is that somethin' personal between you?'

'T'ain't personal,' said Drone. 'T'ain't that private neither. Just an opinion. A reckonin' we share.'

'And what might that be?'

Drone circled the boot cap again. 'This town, this whole place – we ain't sure it's right for us. Look at it. It's just a mess; a big hole. How we goin' to make anythin' here? What we goin' to do? Sit about like leftovers? Shootin' up a few town folk can get a mite borin' to fellas of our kind. And now there's Wilson. There's always Wilson. Always has been. This place ain't goin' to be nothin' 'til he's out of it – for good.'

Scoone settled a dark stare on his partner's face. 'Then mebbe "fellas of your kind" had best go and do what you've been so busy reckonin'. Go find Wilson. Kill him.'

He had been tempted to add 'if you can', but thought better of it and simply smiled when the two men had settled again to a new game of cards.


The clean up and clearing of the street of charred timbers, ash and mud continued through what remained of that night. Buildings were made safe where it was needed. Those beyond any repair were demolished. Sites for repair at some time in the future were earmarked. Men counted their blessings that so much had been saved in the coming of the heavier rain, but berated themselves for the incalculable losses, particularly of lives. A street could be brought back to life; dead men had no such second chance.

116

Little was made of the news that Marshal Wilson was alive and free again. Some already rated him a spent force who would clear the town as fast as he could and stay clear – if he had any sense.

'Mebbe his time will come again,' a town man had concluded. 'But it ain't goin' to be here, not in Random.'

Others were of the opinion that he would ride for help. 'Darnit, he knows our situation here well enough, knows what we're facin'. He ain't goin' to turn his back on us, is he?'

Talk of seeking their own help picked up at the first touch of light. Two youths volunteered to make a run for it to the first town in any direction, and might well have done so had it not been for Pop Ryder's timely intervention.

'Do that and the minute Scoone gets to hear – and he will, rest on that – he'll start killin'. Anybody will do. Them nearest will be the first, then he'll start selectin' like pourin' salt into fresh wounds. Our women, the young girls. . . . Believe me, this bunch we got sittin' on our backs are evil through and through. So save your breath, and your lives, young fellas, and do like the sheriff asks: help restore Random. Don't let it die. We've gotta keep the town alive. It's our only hope.'

News from Pete Phillips at the livery that Wilson's horse and tack had disappeared surprised nobody. The marshal had gone, somehow managing to cope with his wound, and would not be seen again. And who, in their heart of hearts, could blame him? He was a man no longer able to defend himself and only waiting on the day of his execution. He had taken the only option open to him.

Doc Marchman meantime was busy on two fronts. The bereaved, distressed, plain scared, had to be tended and consoled. Wounds had been dressed, minor operations performed, two births tended without a hitch.

He freely admitted to losing Wilson from under his very nose in the heat of the shooting, though Lanky Joe had his doubts about that. He was as certain as made no odds that he had seen Doc helping the marshal to the saloon's back door. Not, of course, that he was prepared to say as much up front. Doc always knew what he was doing by Lanky's reckoning. Even so, he was up to something. . . .

And so he was, and it was going almost exactly to plan.

Doc had explained to the bar girl Alice that one of the ways of ensuring that Scoone did not have things going all his way, was to arm the girls with guns smuggled into their rooms.

'I'm the only soul hereabouts given a free hand to come and go to Patsy's room unquestioned – *and* without bein' searched. And don't forget, my dear, I always have my bag in my hand. . . .'

So far he had managed to smuggle and hide four guns and ammunition in Patsy's room. Two more and there would be enough to arm all the girls in preparation for a time when they would be needed. Quite when that would be he had no idea, but it would happen, of that he was sure.

And so the dawn came up on a day that saw the rain clouds scudding far to the east, a warm, drying breeze blowing in from the south, the fire smoke clearing to drifting wisps, and McKellan's store open for business.

But nothing could conceal the stench of fear and death.

# CHAPTER TWENTY

It was sun-up the following day when Scoone announced he would hang Billy Jay at noon.

He had summoned the town men to present themselves at the front of the saloon and droned his decision in a voice thick with booze, smoke and lack of sleep.

'Noon – you hear that? Sharp on the hour. No messin'. I ain't for messin', you'd best know that. And you'll all be there.' He had flung a loose arm in the general direction of the livery corral. 'There, at the tree. And you'll all watch and learn a lesson: there'll be no more gettin' gun smart with Edrow Scoone or any of his partners ever again. Got it?'

He had grabbed a half-empty bottle of whiskey from Bullets Machin and swilled it liberally over his face. 'And now, if you'll excuse me,' he smirked, swaying unsteadily on his feet. 'I got myself an appointment with one of them pretty bar gals back there. Wouldn't be one bit gentlemanly, would it, to keep her waitin'?'

He had belched through a long gutteral groan, turned, swayed again and, with whiskey streaming like sweat down his dark, stubbled face, disappeared with a stagger through the saloon's batwings.

The town men had dispersed quietly, their faces grey

with the strain of recent days and the prospects to come, their murmurings low and sullen, without hope and, in some cases, without care.

Cuts Bailey, Charlie Mint and Ben McKellan had joined Sheriff Caulk where he had watched from among the burned-out remains of an old barn.

'Fella's booze addled to the back of his brain,' said Cuts, throwing aside a length of charred timber. 'This rate he'll drink himself to death.'

'But not before he's added to the body count around here,' quipped Charlie, his glare watery but defiant. 'And now it's Billy Jay,' he went on, his voice lowering. 'Young fool. Why'd he have to go and do. . . ? Ah, what the hell, all too damned late now. Scoone's here, he's stayin', he's runnin' the place, and there ain't a finger we've got left to lift.'

'Except me,' said Caulk, his gaze still fixed on the saloon.

'What you sayin' there, Sheriff?' asked Ben. 'I hope you ain't reckonin' on—'

'I'm still the law in this town.' Caulk turned his gaze on the town men. 'I wear the badge. I'm legally elected. I represent you, every one of you, charged with my duty to uphold the law and make this town a decent place to live and raise our young 'uns.'

'And there ain't nobody arguin' to that,' said Cuts earnestly. 'You've done a fine job for us. Nobody arguin' to that neither. Darnit, there ain't a fella worth his name who wouldn't back you to the very hilt.'

'Amen to that,' added Charlie.

'Then you're goin' to have to do just that – back me to the hilt,' said Caulk.

'What's that mean exactly?' murmured Ben.

Caulk turned to stare at the saloon again. 'It means, gentlemen, that come noon I'm goin' to be standin' at the old tree in the corral and I ain't movin'.'

News of Sheriff Caulk's intention and his stubborn refusal to hear any talk of not making a stand against Scoone and his henchmen spread quickly, though only in whispers well clear of the Golden Gaze.

Groups of men gathered in the shadows, some in full agreement with the town's elected lawman, others not so sure that a stand would make the slightest difference.

'Fact is,' one man had concluded, 'Scoone'll shoot him right there and then hang Billy Jay. It's the way of things, ain't it?'

An air of resignation to a miserable fate began to settle among the folk, the charred remains of buildings and the fast drying mud. Anger and frustration simmered side by side, but there was no will to risk further shootings with the inevitable body count.

'When you're dealin' with rattlers, you don't go messin' their nest,' a worn old-timer had reckoned.

'But you don't stand there and let 'em bite you!' had been the sharp retort.

Some of the younger men and youths were still for taking more positive lines. 'Mebbe we should stand along of the sheriff,' had been one opinion. 'Darnit, if Caulk's willin' to die for the town, shouldn't we? Scoone can't shoot us all, can he?'

But the general consensus had been that he could and probably would. 'Men like Scoone don't give a damn to a life. He kills to preserve his own and profit from the effort.'

And so the morning had dragged painfully on, with

more eyes turned to clocks and timepieces than almost anything else. Every tick, every clunk to the half-hour and then the hour seemed to sound like the steps of the Grim Reaper himself as men watched, sweated, murmured, waited on Scoone's next move.

It was a little after eleven-fifteen by the saloon clock when Lanky Joe laid aside his glasscloth and went to meet Doc Marchman at the batwings.

'They're all quiet at the moment,' he whispered, one eye on the shadowy far corner of the bar where a ribbon of smoke drifted on the stale, booze-soaked air. 'Halfneck's upstairs with one of the gals. The others are here. They got a game runnin' between themselves.'

Doc nodded. 'Keep a close watch on the rats. Where's Billy Jay?'

'Bound and gagged backroom. He can't take much more.' Lanky glanced anxiously at the far corner. 'Any news? Any sign of Wilson?'

'Nothin'. Don't expect none. Sheriff's all for makin' a stand of it at the corral tree. Figures they'll have to shoot him point blank if they want to hang Billy Jay.'

'Scoone'll do just that!' moaned Lanky.

Doc sighed, held his bag in a firm grip and made for the stairs. Minutes later the door to Patsy Newbutt's room had opened and clicked quietly closed. The last guns had been delivered.

Lanky collected his besom and stepped out to the boardwalk to face a morning that had gathered under a slow, hanging mist as the heat deepened and the sodden earth relented.

Spooky for the time of day, thought Lanky, swishing the besom across the stained, chipped boards. Buildings seemed blurred, grey and ghostly. Shapes were only half formed, some not at all to anything recognizable. And the silence was heavy; an invisible shroud that simply hung, had no beginning and no end.

He stifled a shudder, swished the besom with an added force and was almost grateful for the sound even though it echocd down the empty street like something lost.

The saloon clock struck the half-hour as a signal to Scoone to throw his hand of cards across the table, finish his drink, push back his chair and come to his feet, a leering grin already slithering across his wet lips.

'Time to get organized,' he announced. 'We've got a hangin' waitin' on us!'


The townfolk appeared in the misty street like silent shapes of deeper grey. Some came alone, some in the closer company of neighbours, others in groups – men, women, youngsters – but all at the same, slow pace, heading as if summoned to the livery corral and the hanging tree by an inner voice.

Sheriff Caulk, with Fisty Fox and Joe Dimes at his side, waited at the corral gate, his gaze fixed without blinking on the saloon. Folk shuffled past him. Pop Ryder nodded, but said nothing. Cuts Bailey hovered, uncertain of what to do until Charlie Mint drew him aside.

'This whole thing could explode in our faces any second,' he hissed in Cuts's ear. 'You seen anybody carryin' a gun?'

'Nobody dare risk it,' whispered Cuts. 'Only one armed is the sheriff.' He swallowed tightly. 'Looks as if he's plannin' to do what he said. Hell, he'll be a dead man in minutes. We goin' to let it happen?'

'Can we stop it?'

123

The two fell silent as faces turned and eyes focused on the sight of Billy Jay being thrust through the saloon batwings by Halfneck Quire and Bullets Machin. Scoone and Keefer Drone followed behind them, their hands settled like perching vultures on the butts of holstered Colts.

Scoone paused at the top of the steps from the board-walk to the street and gazed over the faces watching from the other side of the street.

'Just in case anybody's gettin' some fool idea of lettin' the lead fly durin' this operation,' he drawled, 'he'd best be warned.' He gestured to Drone at the 'wings to open them. 'Take a good look what we got here.'

Doc Marchman supported the pale, gaunt figure of Patsy Newbutt to the boardwalk.

Scoone spat into the street dirt. 'I promise you that any man so much as moves against me or my boys, the woman here dies. You got that? It plain as day to you? Good, then we'll proceed.'

They pushed, prodded and occasionally kicked Billy Jay along the street to the livery. The gatherings of town folk followed in silence, eyes tight with anger and deep hatred glaring at every step taken by Scoone and his men.

A youth with a long-bladed knife concealed in his shirt felt the colour rising in his cheeks, a cold, clammy sweat prickling in the back of his neck, his hands wet with nerves. Would he do it? Could he? Dare he? Would he be fast enough? He had the element of surprise on his side. If he moved quickly, got ahead of the others, came closer. . . .

They had reached the corral gates when Scoone called a halt, his gaze fixed on Sheriff Caulk where he stood beneath the spreading reach of the old tree's stoutest bough – the only limb thick enough, sturdy enough to bear the thrashing weight of a hanging man.

'You makin' a point here, Sheriff?' called Scoone through the grey of the still clinging mist. 'You got somethin' to say? Well, you'd best get to it so I can get on with my business here. Now, what's troublin' you, lawman?'

Billy Jay stared and shivered and mouthed silent prayers.

# CHAPTER TWENTY-ONE

Caulk stood his ground, dark against the haunting light. His gaze shifted slowly over the faces watching at the corral gate; town men, their women, their youngsters; ordinary folk in what, until a few days ago, had been an ordinary settlement.

Now it was a ghost town, except that here the ghosts were living.

'I'm waitin', Sheriff,' called Scoone again.

Billy Jay fought to control his shivering. Patsy Newbutt leaned against Doc as if about to melt into the mist. The town folk stared. The bar girls hugged themselves in dampening shawls. Lanky Joe had left the saloon still holding his besom. The youth with the knife in his shirt had come within a lunge of Keefer Drone.

'There'll be no lynchin' in this town,' boomed Caulk, his voice thickening as it travelled.

'That so?' quipped Scoone. He spat into a lifeless pool of rainwater, then nodded to Quire and Machin to move ahead with Billy Jay between them.

'You hear me, Scoone? I said there'll be no lynchin'.'

'I hear you, lawman. But I don't figure for your word

countin' for a whole lot right now. I mean, this ain't your town no more, is it? You're wearin' the badge, Sheriff, but you ain't the law.'

Caulk remained still and silent, a trickle of his breath drifting to oblivion in the mist. Quire and Machin halted, their grips tight on Billy Jay's shaking body. Doc Marchman cradled Patsy's head on his shoulder; Lanky Joe's knuckles whitened on the besom handle. The town folk continued to stare. Smoke slipped timelessly from the forge. A stabled horse snorted. Silence brooded.

'I'll give you two minutes to be clear of that tree,' said Scoone, his eyes narrowing on the sheriff. 'Two minutes, lawman, no more. So why don't you step aside now and make it easy?' He wiped the back of his hand across his mouth. 'I ain't for killin' you, but I will, oh, yes, I surely will.'

Nobody moved, nobody spoke. The youth with the knife slid his hand inside his shirt and flexed his fingers round the handle. He was still close to Drone; close enough to strike and bury the long blade deep in the man's back. All he had to do. . . .

'Time's tickin', lawman,' called Scoone.

'Don't do it, Sheriff. Just back off,' muttered Cuts Bailey to himself.

'He won't,' answered Charlie Mint like an echo. 'Darn fool will die where he stands.'

'It's all a waste, a terrible waste. . . .'

The youth made his move in a sudden, thrusting lunge that propelled his body over the still sticky ground into the bulk of Keefer Drone.

But he had failed in his excitement and anxiety to take a full grip on the knife and pull it from inside his shirt. The result was chaos.

Drone staggered forward for a moment, regained his balance, swung round, his Colt already clearing leather, and recognized instantly the look of crazed madness glazed with panic in the young man's eyes. He swiped the barrel of the Colt across the youth's head to send him spinning through the dirt like blown trash.

The knife, now tight in the youth's grip and clear of his shirt, gleamed menacingly but only for as long as it took for Drone's boot to thud across his wrist and pin it to the ground.

'Rat!' seethed Drone, levelling his Colt for the fatal blaze.

'No! Wait!' roared Scoone. 'He can hang along of the other.'

Drone dragged the youth to his feet, ripped a sleeve from his shirt to bind his wrists and pushed him forward to join Billy Jay.

'Gettin' to be one helluva party, ain't it?' leered Scoone, his wet gaze gleaming as he scanned the faces of the town folk. 'Anybody else for joinin' in? Who fancies his chances, eh? Step forward now. Don't be shy!'

Cuts Bailey stiffened. 'For two pins. . . .' he hissed, but relaxed again under Charlie Mint's restraining hand.

'No offers?' scoffed Scoone. 'Beginnin' to see sense, eh? Very wise. That way you stay breathin'.'

'Let's get on with this, shall we?' grumbled Drone. 'We're wastin' good time. Could be back there in the saloon enjoyin' them gals along with the booze.'

Lanky Joe gripped the besom in both hands. If he had his way, he thought, Scoone and his sidekicks would die of thirst. A long, slow, painful death.

'You hear that, Sheriff?' shouted Scoone, switching his gaze to where Caulk still stood his ground at the tree.

'We're gettin' kinda impatient down here, so if you're goin' to make a move, you'd best be gettin' on with it.'

Scoone led his party forward. Billy Jay continued to stumble and shudder under the prodding and shoving of Machin and Quire. The youth fell in his wake, his face glistening under a lathering of cold sweat, his limbs suddenly as soft as sodden paper.

Scoone spoke softly out of the corner of his mouth to Bullets Machin. 'Few more yards then you can lift that Winchester of yours and put that squawkin' sheriff down. I don't want him dead. Not yet. Just make sure he ain't troublesome for a while.'

Machin grinned, grunted and prodded the rifle barrel into Billy Jay's back. 'Be a pleasure,' he grunted.

The steps slowed under Scoone's watchful pace. 'Now,' he said, spreading his arms as he halted.

There was no more than the faintest twitch from Sheriff Caulk in the split seconds between Machin's Winchester levelling and the shot being fired.

Caulk spun to his left, tried to lay a grip on his Colt, but could only grab at his shoulder as blood oozed steadily between his fingers and a throbbing wound burned like fire.

Scoone spat again, grunted and moved on. Doc Marchman eased Patsy to the care of the bar girls, adjusted his hat and the set of his coat and mouthed a long curse. 'S'cuse me,' he murmured, 'looks like I'm needed.'

'Sonofabitch,' hissed Lanky through a stream of hot white breath.

Cuts Bailey clenched his fists. 'I ain't standin' for this. Goddamnit, that rat thinks he can do just anythin' takes his fancy. Well, I ain't for takin' it. I'm tellin' you—'

'Easy, easy,' soothed Charlie Mint. 'You want to join

them two about to get their necks stretched? Wouldn't take a deal for Scoone to have a real hangin' hoedown here. Don't give him the chance.'

'But we can't just let this happen.'

'Don't look to me there's a deal we can do, unless you wanna start a bloodbath.'

A handful of town men on the far side of the corral gate began to shuffle and move forward slowly as a body. One of them – a heavily built fellow with a bristling moustache and bushy sideburns – carried a pick handle and moved with the authority of a self-appointed leader.

'Enough's enough,' he growled, eyeing Cuts, Charlie and Lanky Joe. 'Them scum are goin' to string up two of our own, f'chris'sake. Ain't there been enough dyin'?'

'Hold it,' said Ben McKellan, easing his way through the gathering. 'If we get to rushin' at Scoone, they'll take us out simple as spittin' pips from a berry. We gotta think of somethin' else. There has to be another way.'

'Only way I know—' began the heavy town fellow, but was cut short as a gasp went up from the watching folk.

'Too late,' groaned Charlie. 'Them boys'll be swingin' dead inside a couple of minutes.'

Billy Jay and the youth had been mounted on wooden crates beneath the menacing reach of the tree's long bough from which two ropes hung, the nooses loose on the men's necks.

Sheriff Caulk, with Doc squatting at his side, glared defiantly but uselessly at Scoone as he lit a cigar, waited for the glow to deepen, blew smoke and twisted his lips in his familiarly cynical manner.

'It's like I told you,' he said from behind the smoke, 'folk have to learn. They gotta know who's boss, what's what – no messin', just straight up doin' like you're told and behavin' decent to them who make the rules.'

'I'll see you in Hell!' winced Caulk.

'Well, that's a very fair possibility, my friend,' grinned Scoone. 'But that ain't now, is it? That ain't as things stand this minute. Nothin' like. So let's be realistic, eh? Make the most of what we got. And if we have to do it the hard way. . . .'

The thudding rush of pounding hoofs came through the mist like some phantom sound out of nightmare.

The drone of Scoone's voice died instantly. Doc Marchman came slowly to his feet and stared into the still clinging wall of mist.

'What in the name of hell is that?' mouthed Quire.

Bullets Machin levelled his Winchester, his grip suddenly sticky. Keefer Drone stood back from the hanging ropes and squinted for a shape to identify the sound.

The pounding came on, deeper, closer, consuming the silence.

'Rider comin' in. Fast,' grated Quire.

'You see him?' asked Machin, steadying his rifle.

'Not yet.'

Scoone let the cigar slip from between his fingers and sizzle on the sodden ground. His eyes narrowed. His lips dried.

The townsfolk stood without a movement among them, without a word between them, listening, watching, wondering just who or what it was out there beyond the curtain of mist.

Charlie Mint squinted, peered, widened his eyes till he thought they would pop, but saw nothing. Cuts Bailey at his side felt a deepening chill down his spine. Pop Ryder murmured, 'Oh, my,' and sensed his body go limp.

'Well, don't just stand there gawpin' like girls, do somethin', f'chris'sake!' cursed Scoone.

Bullets Machin raised his Winchester, levelled and steadied it on a target he could only hear and had taken the trigger pressure when a roar and a blaze burst through the mist like the anger of a storm in Hell.

The air seemed to come alive, to be swished aside as a rider, dark, tall in the saddle, reins in one hand, a rifle in the other, descended on the corral, urged his mount over the fence and pounded towards the hanging tree as if intent on ripping it from the ground.

The rider's gun blazed again, this time lifting Machin off the ground and throwing him to land face-down in the soggy dirt.

Scoone flung himself aside, sprawling in a heap at the side of Keefer Drone. Halfneck Quire lost his footing and toppled back as if felled by a giant club.

The rider brought his horse round in a swishing, swirling half-circle, let it gather itself for a moment then pounded back to the tree. His rifle blazed through a hail of shots, scattering earth in a dirt storm. Quire made a bid to grab his Colt from its holster only to yell out with pain as a bullet streaked clean through his hand, spouting his own blood into his face.

Doc Marchman, bent double, wobbling on unsteady legs, made what he could of a dash to slip the nooses clear of Billy Jay and the youth, fumble to release their bound wrists and bark at them to scatter.

The rider passed the tree, fired high into the air and charged away, clearing the distant fence in a flying leap before disappearing deep into the mist.

Minutes later the townfolk had scattered back to the safety, the closeness and concealment of the town, and

Scoone, Keefer Drone and Halfneck Quire hurried as fast as they could to the saloon.

They left the dead body of Bullets Machin where it lay in the dirt.

# CHAPTER TWENTY-TWO

'It was Wilson. Must've been. There ain't nobody else – leastways, nobody fool enough to risk what he did.' The town man drew gently on a freshly lit cheroot and savoured the intake before blowing the smoke to what remained of the roof of the fire ravaged barn. 'Pity of it is, he didn't finish it.'

'He couldn't, though, could he?' said Pop Ryder, helping himself to a swig from his much prized but battered hip flask. 'He was bleedin' from that wound by the time he turned for the second charge. All he could do, from where I was standin', to get clear.'

A moon-faced young fellow with a stream of yellow hair brushing his shoulders sank his hands deep into the pockets of his dungarees. 'But, hell, he sure left his mark, didn't he? Did you see the way that scumbag Bullets Machin hit the dirt? He flew, blown clean off his feet, almost out of his boots – then, wham, flat on his back like a booze-soaked slug. I ain't seen a fella die like that before. Not never. Wow – must've been some shot, eh? That was real shootin'.'

'Mebbe,' said Charlie Mint, pushing his hat clear of his

brow, 'but we're still stranded, ain't we? I mean, Billy Jay and that kid are free and alive, but Scoone's back in the saloon with them other two rats. Back there and still callin' the shots while ever he's got Lanky, the gals and Miss Patsy.'

A short man with a squint in one eye scuffed his boot through wet ash. 'Should never have let Scoone get back to the saloon,' he grunted. 'Should've stopped 'em there and then.'

'How?' asked Cuts Bailey sharply. 'Tell me just how when Drone had grabbed Patsy and rounded up them gals faster than spittin' bad meat. It's Drone who's the smart one if you ask me. He realized quick enough it's the females holdin' the keys to the saloon. Without them, Scoone had no place to run. Now, like you say, he's back. And this time he's goin' to take a whole heap of shiftin', mark my words.'

The moon-faced fellow frowned. 'Well, who knows, mebbe he'll see the writin's on the wall for him as far as this town bein' a place to retire to. Hell, the way I see it he ain't goin' to get much peaceful livin' hereabouts! Nossir he ain't. Damn it, he's seen half the town go up in smoke; he's left one of his sidekicks dead in the dirt back there, and another's out of gun-totin' action for the time bein'. That don't look none too healthy now, does it? And that ain't mentionin' the fact that there's a hate-spittin' marshal close by all set to haunt him 'til he's dead. Call that retirement?'

The town men nodded and murmured their agreement.

'Fella's right,' said Pop Ryder. 'It's Wilson who's goin' to settle this one way or the other.'

'It sure as sun-up ain't goin' to be Sheriff Caulk,' piped

a man perched on a charred crate. 'He's in a bad way so I hear. Which leaves Wilson, don't it? Just Wilson. Ain't nobody else.'

'There's us,' said Charlie. 'Damn it, we're still here. This is still our town.'

A lean man scratched his head. 'I ain't so sure about that, Charlie. It *was* our town 'til Scoone rode in. Fact is, there's plenty – Smack Evans, Slippy Jones and his missus, the Kettles, Jonas Brigg, widow Hartshaw, Angus Castle and them two good-lookin' gals of his, Pete Mullery – a whole crowd of 'em all set for pullin' out soon as they can.'

'And I heard tell only this evenin' after all that shootin' at the corral as how Spots Ringer and his whole family are plannin' to shift West,' said the moon-faced fellow.

'What, all fifteen of 'em?' gulped Cuts.

'S'right. Spots, the missus – who's bulgin' again – and the thirteen young 'uns. Takes some swallowin', don't it?'

'But we can't permit that to happen,' said Ben McKellan, stepping from the shadows into the glow of the single lantern. 'Such folk are the future of Random, of the whole territory. Lose them and we'll be a ghost town in no time. Just dead wood, cobwebs, an empty street, somewhere that simply gave up.'

'Over my dead body!' said Charlie, almost choking on the words. 'No, we ain't for givin' up. We've come this far and we'll keep goin'.'

But there was no voice raised to suggest how.


Halfneck Quire slopped a measure of whiskey to his glass from the bottle held in his shaking grip, cursed, sank the drink and stared at the bulk of bandaging burying his gun hand.

Keefer Drone blew a thin stream of cigar smoke to the

stained ceiling of the Golden Gaze saloon, shifted his position in the chair facing Quire and grinned. 'You can watch it all you like, fella, t'ain't goin' to heal it no faster than comes natural.' He drummed his fingers on the table between the two men. 'Question you got to be askin' yourself is: how long before I can fire a piece again? T'ain't an encouragin' prospect from here.'

Quire wiped his mouth on the back of his good hand. 'I was thinkin' about Bullets,' he droned. 'Could've been any one of us who took that lead. You, me, Edrow there. We got lucky.'

'And you got 'specially lucky,' quipped Drone. 'Wilson could've shot you any part of your body he chose. Fact is, he could've—'

'I've heard all I want to hear of Wilson for one day,' snapped Scoone, moving from the shadows to the soft glow of lantern light. 'He's a pain, real naggin', back of my head. No more talk of him, right? Losin' Bullets is bad enough.'

'Can't bury Wilson, though, can we?' said Drone. 'He's still here some place; still waitin' on us makin' a move.'

Quire poured another measure. 'Should've let that hangin' business pass. Should've stayed low, stayed quiet. Mebbe we should never have hit this two-bit town. Just kept ridin'. Gone south, crossed the border.' He sank the drink and licked at the dribbles glistening in the corners of his mouth. 'Can't say I'm for retirin' anyhow.'

Scoone crossed to the table and thudded his fist in the whiskey stains. 'We agreed.' he thundered. 'The four of us. We were through, ready for our own place, our own town, a town just like this.' He leaned closer to glare into Quire's eyes. 'We're here now, this *is* our town, save for cleanin' that mess on our doorstep name of Wilson. So we will. You bet.'

'How?' asked Drone, drumming his fingers again. 'How we goin' to clean up Wilson? He's nobody's fool. He's been trackin' us like forever. He's a hauntin'. He's here, there . . . wherever we seem to turn. And now, he's kinda got us penned, ain't he? I mean, we've walked into this of our own free will. Chose the town. Chose the time. Rode in, took over this saloon.' His eyes darkened. 'And if we ain't awful careful, partner, it ain't goin' to be no more than a prison cell. So show me the keys, eh? Show me.'

Lanky Joe stood up from behind the bar, wiped his hands down the front of his apron and poured himself a stiff drink which he sank with barely a gulp in one deep swallow.

He had heard every word spoken between Scoone and his sidekicks, and for the first time detected a note of doubt in their voices, particularly in the case of Keefer Drone. He was getting uncertain; not anxious and far from scared, but unsure of just where the three men were heading. And the threat of Marshal Wilson had seemed to darken across their horizon like a storm cloud. Halfneck Quire was right: the attempted showpiece hanging of Billy Jay and the youth had been a mistake.

But what would Scoone do now? Would he plan for a showdown with Wilson? The marshal had sustained a bad wound. How bad? Would he wait before making another close contact? If he did – and with Sheriff Caulk out of action – where did that leave the townfolk? That was as far as Lanky's thoughts went as Scoone crossed to the bar, demanded a fresh bottle of whiskey and shouted from the foot of the stairs for the girls to get themselves down there right now. 'What about that Newbutt gal?' he asked.

'Doc said when he left a while back as how the young

miss was sleepin' sound and was not to be disturbed,' said Lanky, with a flourish of his glasscloth across the counter. 'His very words.'

Scoone grunted and peered into the shadowy flight of stairs.

'Where's them girls? They deaf or somethin'? Have I got to fetch 'em m'self?'

He had a foot on the stairs and was about to begin the climb when he swung round at the sound of approaching hoofbeats. He heard them gather, strengthen, draw nearer, until they were pounding through the darkness like thunder.

No one in the saloon moved or seemed to breathe as the hoofbeats slithered through the street dirt to a halt. A heavy weight thudded to the boardwalk beyond the batwings. A horse snorted, tack jangled; the hoofbeats began again, fading now into the silence of the empty night.

Keefer Drone was the first to move.

He came to his feet slowly, watchfully, his gaze fixed on the 'wings, the pitch blackness beyond them. A minute, nearer two, passed before he moved again, his steps measured, almost silent on the bar's boot-bitten floor-boards.

'Go easy there,' urged Quire, leaning forward.

'You bet,' murmured Drone.

Scoone stood in silence, his eyes shifting like sudden flames from Drone to Quire, to Lanky Joe, then, as they darkened, to the 'wings. His fingers moved as if with a life of their own to the butt of his holstered Colt. An unseen movement, a sudden noise, and the piece would clear leather and blaze with the speed of a blink.

Lanky Joe swallowed. No mistaking in his mind the

rider out there had been Wilson. The hoofbeats had been the same as those he had heard earlier approaching the corral; the same assured beat, the same depth and strength. The marshal was still here. And now maybe Scoone could feel it in his very bones.

Drone reached the 'wings, stepped to one side and peered into the street. 'Hell,' he groaned, relaxing.

'What's there, f'chris'sake?' hissed Scoone.

'Bullets. Somebody's dumped his body right here.'

'Wilson!' growled Scoone.

Drone pushed open the 'wings. 'I don't doubt it was Wilson. Gotta be. Only he would have the guts for it. It's always Wilson. Everythin' is that sonofabitch, snake-slith-erin'— Hold on, there's a paper here, fixed to the body. There's writin'.'

'Can you read it?' said Scoone.

' 'Course I can read it. I ain't no dumbhead.'

'What's it say?'

There was a pause, a silence through which only the bar clock ticked on effortlessly.

'Well?' urged Scoone.

'It just says "Sun Up",' said Drone, stepping back into the bar light with the paper in his hands. 'Just that: "Sun Up". No more. But I guess it don't take much figurin', does it?'

# CHAPTER
# TWENTY-THREE

Any number of town men, their heads still buzzing with the events of the day, had been about late enough that night to witness Wilson's hair-raising ride through the street. But only Ben McKellan could lay claim to a first-hand, close-up encounter.

'Saw it all, darn near clear as day you might say,' he told a group gathered on the boardwalk outside the sheriff's office. 'I was there, in the store, still tryin' to clear up the mess from the fire and doin' the best I could to get back to—'

'Yeah, yeah,' clipped a man in the shadows. 'Just get to it, will you? Tell us what you saw.'

'I kinda heard it first,' the storekeeper began again. 'That same low rumblin' we heard at the corral. A rider comin' in – not so fast as before, but steady enough and direct. Couldn't be headin' no place save the street, so I stepped outside. Hard to see anythin' much from the single light at the store. I figured I'd get a whole sight better view of who was comin' from the other side. Saloon was lit up. There weren't nobody about – none that I could see – just the sounds; voices from the bar and them hoofbeats, gettin' louder.' Ben paused, conscious now of a heavily bandaged Sheriff Caulk, his deputies, and Doc Marchman watching from the open door to the office.

'Time I'd got myself settled far side of the 'wings where it was too dark to be noticed, the rider was almost there. Then I saw him. Saw his face, that stare in his eyes. Saw the sweat gleamin' in the scar he carries. No mistakin' – it was Wilson, and he didn't seem to be sufferin' none from that wound. He had a body slung across the mount. It was that scumbag Bullets Machin.'

Ben paused again, this time to swallow and flick his gaze across the faces of those listening to him. 'Everythin' seemed to happen together then. Wilson slowed the horse, reined back hard, halted, flung the body across the boardwalk, stared at it for a second, then rode on. He went down the street like somethin' out of Hell itself and was out of sight when Drone crashed through the 'wings and stood starin' at the body like he was seein' a ghost. It was the note – a scrap of paper with writin' on it fixed to Machin's body – that held Drone's attention 'til that madman Scoone yelled out from the bar for him to tell him what the hell was happenin'.'

'Did you see what was written on the paper?' asked Caulk.

'No, I was too far away and it was too dark. But I heard, sure enough. All it said was "Sun Up". I heard Drone say it twice. "Sun Up".'

'That's plain enough for me,' said Pop Ryder. 'No messin'. Wilson's for a showdown, and he's given Scoone the time of it. Sun up is when the lawman will ride in.'

'Hell,' groaned a town man, 'that means more lead flyin', more blood, more bodies.'

'Will Scoone wait at the saloon?' asked another. 'Him

and Drone and that shot-up sidekick Quire. You reckon they'll all be there waitin' on just one man?'

'They'll be there,' said Charlie Mint. 'Safest place they can hole-up, ain't it? And while ever they're there they'll still have the gals and Miss Patsy. Scoone'll use them some-how, you can bet to it.'

Doc's eyes glinted behind the soft smile to himself. 'And they'll have me,' he murmured. 'I'll be there. Goin' to be needed, ain't I?'

Nobody in Random was much for sleeping that night. News of Wilson's ride, the note fixed to the body and the consequences almost certain to follow a showdown spread among the townfolk within minutes of Ben McKellan's eye-witness account. Some men, especially those with family, went to their homes on the promise of not setting foot outside again until the shooting, whatever the outcome, was over. Some men returned to barricade themselves behind locked and bolted doors and prepare for departure at the first chance that presented itself.

Others – mainly the single men and more high-spirited youths – were all for being right there when the lead started to fly.

'Fact of it is,' one man had insisted, 'we might never see the likes again. This'll be the biggest shoot-out the town will see. And could be the biggest in the whole darned territory. It'll be history bein' written right in front of your very eyes.'

Still others argued another approach. 'But what about the gals in the saloon and Miss Patsy? What about Lanky? Then there's Doc. He's goin' to be holed-up at the heart of it, ain't he?'

'And what about Wilson?' Cuts Bailey had counselled. 'I

don't hear a deal bein' said for him. He's goin' to be alone. There ain't goin' to be another gun standin' to him, not unless one of us. . . .'

But there had been no one willing to commit himself to the marshal's side, save Billy Jay who was 'fit for havin' another go' until shouted down by wiser heads.

A tired Sheriff Caulk had stepped from his office again to warn against any man getting involved in the shoot-out. 'This, so far as Random is concerned, is a law matter,' he had told the men, 'and I'm the law in spite of this darned shoulder wound. If anybody hereabouts is to stand to Wilson's side, it'll be me. That's my job. That's why I carry the badge and get paid for doin' so.' He had winced at the throb of the pain in his shoulder. 'Time you were all off the street anyhow. It's gettin' late and there ain't no good bein' served. . . .'

But his words had been lost in the mêlée of voices.

The lantern in the Golden Gaze had been trimmed so that the light was low and faint and the shadows deeper and thicker.

Halfneck Quire had remained seated at his table throughout Wilson's visit. Now he was alone with his thoughts and the numbing pain in his hand. But it would not have taken a deal to bring him to his feet to go in search of his horse at the livery, saddle up and ride out of Random, never to look back or want to see it again. As it was, he knew he would stay just like he had always stayed at Scoone's side almost since he could remember.

And when the showdown with Wilson happened, in the gathering glare of sun up, he would be ready, as ever, to be the unseen gun, the hidden gunslinger whose weapon would blaze at the first hint of Scoone losing ground. It had been that way for as long as he had ridden at Scoone's side. Sun up tomorrow would be no different.

For Keefer Drone there was no time for contemplation. He was for reckoning and figuring fast.

'You goin' out there to face him?' he asked, pacing the length of the saloon, a half-empty bottle of whiskey in his hand. 'You figure the street to be the ground?'

He stared watchfully at Scoone, noting the set of his hands flat on the table in front of him, the poured measure within reach, an unopened pack of cards at the centre.

'Mebbe,' said Scoone without lifting his eyes. 'We'll see.'

'Best decide it now. Don't give Wilson an edge. Choose your own ground, that's always been my way. And the light. You want that early light at your back. Always at your back.'

Scoone raised his wet gaze. 'You think I ain't done this before or somethin'? You're soundin' like some old-timer preachin' to a kid.'

'I'm only sayin', that's all. Just remindin' you.' Drone turned in his pacing and halted, his back to the batwings. 'Can't afford no slip-up this time, not with a man like Wilson. And don't go reckonin' on the shoulder wound slowin' him down. It ain't so far, and it won't. But we wanna be standin' when it's all done. Standin' and breathin'. And we want that law-rat off our backs once and for all. Dead – we want him dead as it gets. I want to see him die, you hear? See it with my own eyes.'

He swigged from the bottle and glared at Lanky Joe where he hovered behind the bar. 'And you, fella, and them gals of yours can stand witness to it all. Understand? You watch and see everythin' just as it happens.' He grinned. 'Then we'll all have a party, eh? A real hoedown of a wake to celebrate Wilson's death. Yessir!'

The night crept silently on.

# CHAPTER
# TWENTY-FOUR

There was still an hour to sun-up when Doc Marchman put the finishing touches to the dressing and bandaging of Sheriff Caulk's shoulder wound, washed his hands in the water bowl, dried them and poured two mugs of fresh coffee.

'Best I can do for now,' he said, offering a mug to the sheriff, 'but I ain't happy at you figurin' for gettin' involved in all this. You ain't fit enough, and you certainly ain't goin' to be able to handle a gun.'

'Can Wilson?' said Caulk sharply, his gaze steady on Doc's face.

Doc hesitated a moment. He sipped the steaming coffee. 'You saw him at the corral.'

'You know what I'm talkin' about, Doc. I'm talkin' about a shoot-out, an all-time, blazin' showdown – a gunfight such as none of us has seen before. There ain't goin' to be any quarter given; no half measures. It's all or nothin'. Scoone don't have no choice, nor does Wilson.' He paused. 'Am I right?'

Doc crossed to the window. 'You're right,' he said, peering into the street where the last of the night was giving way to a pale dawn. 'But as for Wilson bein' fit for a gunfight, who's to say? I can't. A showdown is in a man's mind, and when a mind is set on a destiny like a gunfight to the death, a mere shoulder wound ain't goin' to change it. Wilson's been waitin' for this day for years. He won't ride away now.'

Caulk lit a cheroot and blew the smoke in a thin white line to the ceiling. 'So where does that leave a sheriff?' he asked. 'Don't you think my mind's set? I got a town and its folk to look to here, Doc. Do you think a mere shoulder wound is goin' to put me off doin' my job?'

Doc turned slowly from the window. 'Not for one minute, I don't.' A faint smile flickered at his lips. 'Time I was movin', anyhow. Young Patsy will be expectin' me.'

'You watch your back in that saloon, you hear? Keep your head down and stay clear of the shootin'. Same goes for Lanky and the gals.'

Doc finished his coffee, reached for his coat and bag and closed the office door behind him as he stepped to the boardwalk. He breathed deeply on the clean morning air and turned to gaze into the breaking eastern skies. The day would be clear and bright – for those who lived to see it.

Lanky Joe's besom swept over the same square foot of boardwalk for the fifth time and came to a scratching halt. This was no way to go about what should have been a serious job of work, he thought, with a deep sigh and a tired blink of his eyes.

But what the hell – nothing was as it should be on a morning like this when all a fellow could do was simply stand about, or drift aimlessly from task to task finishing none of them and with no heart to begin again. This was a morning for waiting, watching, listening and, worst of all, picturing what was coming.

He took a step forward and swished the besom again.

How long now, he wondered; fifteen, twenty minutes, a half-hour at best before Wilson appeared? But from which direction would he come? On foot or mounted? Would he call Scoone out? How would he – how could he – cope with the remaining sidekicks? Would Scoone hold Patsy Newbutt under threat of death? Would he threaten to murder the girls, one by one, unless Wilson backed off, or did he want to lay the ghost of him once and for all?

Lanky gripped the besom until his knuckles whitened.

Darn fool questions! Why plague his head with them when he had no answers? Why even bother? His thoughts faded at the sight of Doc making his way down the street through the cling of the low morning mist.

'All quiet in there?' asked Doc when he reached the boardwalk fronting the saloon.

'Ain't nobody sleepin' if that's what you mean,' said Lanky. 'Ain't nobody slept a wink I'd wager. The gals are upstairs. Alice says as how Patsy's calm enough. Keefer Drone is pacing about like a leopard with itchy paws. That fella Quire is starin' at his bound hand like he's expectin' it to explode, and Scoone's just sittin' there, waitin'.'

Lanky glanced quickly at the batwings and lowered his voice. 'You take care in there. Them scumbags are in a twitchy mood. Wouldn't take more than a word to spark 'em. Go easy.'

Doc grunted, took a fresh grip on his bag and pushed open the 'wings.

The worn besom swished, scratched, fell to a softer rhythm as Lanky's concentration settled on the street. The low mist clung like a grey drifting shroud above the rutted mud and packed dirt: the early light crept eerily among the shapes of the burned-out buildings. There were no faces he could see, no sounds he could recognize. He might, he thought, have been marooned in some abandoned town.

Except, damn it, that this was Random.

He cursed softly under his breath and swished the besom defiantly. The town was still alive, still ready to thrive and grow and be a decent place for decent folk to lead decent lives, and if Scoone and his two-bit cronies figured on. . . .

He froze where he stood, the besom silent at his feet, his eyes widening, watering as he watched the mist and listened to the soft swish of the hoofs of an approaching rider.

Lanky swallowed. 'Hell,' he murmured, as if releasing the fear gathering deep in his gut. He swallowed again, felt the sudden pinch of a cold sweat in his neck. 'Hell.' The besom twitched, Lanky blinked and began to shuffle back to the 'wings, conscious of Drone watching the street from the shadowed gloom of the bar.

The rider came on, taking shape now on the light and the still clinging mist, his body steady, his gaze fixed ahead.

'Inside,' hissed Drone, easing open a 'wing.

Lanky hesitated, every sense concentrated on the rider, the slow approach, rhythmic swish of hoofs, occasional creak of leather, the soft tinkle of tack.

'I said inside,' growled Drone.

'Sure,' murmured Lanky, his gaze still fixed, watching every movement, flicking to the shift of a shadow on the opposite boardwalk, the shape of a town man scurrying from cover to cover in a fire-ravaged building.

Lanky eased through the open 'wing and blinked on the smoke-hazed gloom of the saloon. Scoone was on his feet, standing to his full height, twin Colts low slung at his waist. A slight beading of sweat gleamed like a shaking of salt on his stubble.

'You up to handlin' a piece?' he said, addressing Halfneck Quire without looking at him.

'You bet,' said the sidekick, skimming a wince from his face as he came to his feet.

'Time's come. Get to it. Usual place. And don't, f'chris'sake, miss!' Scoone turned his attention to Drone. 'Where's he now?'

'Reined back, middle of the street,' said Drone. 'He ain't movin'. Just watchin'.'

'Anybody with him?'

'He's alone.'

Scoone licked his lips. 'Let him stew for a while, then I'm goin' out. You cover my back, right?'

Drone moved away from the 'wings. 'You want I should get the gal? Wilson wouldn't risk shootin' a woman.'

'Leave her be,' snapped Scoone. 'We may need her later.' He reached for a bottle of whiskey, drained the dregs in a single gulp and thudded the bottle back on the table.

'Get me a fresh one,' he ordered, glaring quickly at Lanky.

Drone hooked his thumbs in his belt. 'Go easy on that juice,' he quipped.

Scoone grunted, licked his lips then aimed a line of spittle to the nearest spittoon. 'Mebbe I'll get this over with right now. I ain't for wastin'—'

'Hold it,' said Drone, stepping back to the 'wings and easing one aside to give him a view of the street.

151

'Sonofabitch!' he hissed. 'He ain't there. He's moved. Just hitched the horse and gone. Disappeared!'

'What in the name of hell is he. . . ?' began Scoone, joining Drone at the 'wings. 'What's his figurin', f'chris'sake?'

Both men slid to the shadowed depths of the boardwalk, their eyes flicking to the left, to the right, back again.

Scoone drew a Colt and edged towards the street. 'If that scumbag of a lawman—'

Three rapid shots spat across the timbers at Scoone's feet, forcing him back in a tangle of legs to the 'wings, where he stumbled and reached blindly for support.

Drone emerged from the shadows, his eyes lit like coals as they scanned the street, the charred buildings opposite for some sign, a shape, the slightest movement to indicate Wilson's presence. There was nothing. He levelled the Colt in his right hand, steadied his grip and fired wildly into no more than empty space.

'Get yourself out here, lawman!' he shouted, blazing another shot. 'Show yourself, or you plannin' on skulkin' there 'til—'

The roar of the marshal's Winchester from somewhere deep in the shell of what had once been the town grain store, lifted Drone clean off his feet to send him crashing through the saloon's front window in a shower of broken glass, flying shards, splinters of timber and an echoing yell of pain.

A second shot hit him before he had fallen, spiralling him in a twist of legs and arms and dancing hair until he finally hit the floor of the bar. He did not move again.

Scoone took one look at the dead man, spat and cursed. 'Halfneck,' he shouted from the foot of the stairs, 'what you seein'? You got a fix on that marshal yet?'

'Nothin',' called the sidekick.

'He's got Drone. He's dead. I'm goin' out there. You keep your eyes peeled.' Scoone swung round to face Lanky where he hovered behind the bar, the besom tight in his grip. 'And you, fella, get this place cleaned up. You hear me? I want it lookin' shiny as a polished barrel. We'll be havin' a party here when I'm all through with that law rat.' He glanced at the body again. 'Keefer would've wanted that. He was always one for a party.' Scoone's gaze dampened for a moment before he stiffened, checked the set of the twin Colts at his waist and moved steadily through the shafting light to the batwings.

'This won't take long,' he murmured, but not to Lanky or to Halfneck Quire.

He was addressing the dead man.

# CHAPTER TWENTY-FIVE

Scoone was still talking to himself in a low, toneless mumble that shaped only sounds, when he stepped through the batwings and let them creak shut behind him.

The morning had grown clearer, whiter, with a rich blue sky settling fast. The sun, though not yet at its full height, had deepened and stretched the shadows so that they lay across the earth like black bars. The mist had drifted away, but the silence remained unbroken, tensed, as if listening to itself.

Scoone's gaze flicked quickly from the street to his right, to the sprawl of buildings to his left. It missed nothing. Twenty years of harsh survival, near misses, lucky escapes and a blade-sharp shrewdness had taught him all he needed to know about shadows, dark alleys and the seemingly impossible places a man might hide. He had once boasted he could smell a gun at a hundred yards and spot a killer in fifty – but that had been when he was a younger man; the new blood on the scene that was never challenged.

Today, he was mumbling.

'Sonofabitch'll pay for shootin' Keefer like that, and

Bullets. Ain't a man livin' can do that to me – take out my two best guns – and stay breathin'.' The level of his voice lifted. 'You hearin' me, Wilson? You'd better be. You're the one payin' for all this. Yessir. . . . You can bet to it. . . .'

Scoone had shifted barely a dozen relaxed steps along the boardwalk. But slow and casual as they might have seemed, his eyes, his senses were working at a pace, and his fingers never more than a whisper clear of the butts of his Colts.

He thought he had a notion now as to where Wilson had hidden himself.

'Tell you this, Marshal, I ain't for waitin' another minute on this cat-and-mouse show,' he called, reaching the deepest of the boardwalk's shadows. 'I'm for killin' you, and you, I guess, are for *tryin'* to kill me. Well, go ahead, make your bid, step out into the street there where I can see you and we'll soon know who's got the edge. But I warn you, Wilson, I'm fast . . . oh, yes, real fast. I've shot a whole sight better men than you before takin' my first sup of the day. Why, I recall. . . .' The voice rambled on, drifting from the darkly menacing to the almost jovial; in one minute a deadly growl, in the next a light-hearted banter behind a fit of tittering.

The street's stillness hung like a curtain. If there were eyes watching – and there must have been – they, too, stayed hidden.

'Might've figured for lettin' you out of this, Marshal, if it hadn't been for Bullets and Keefer. Mebbe we could've done a deal. Damn it, you ain't gettin' any younger. Like me, you're mebbe for retirin', hangin' up the gunbelt, eh? Well, this place, this town, is my retirement, Mr Lawman Wilson, and I ain't for changin' plans now, so I suggest. . . .'

Scoone's voice faded. He had heard the step at his back, the softest creak of a timber board, the tread of a man who already had the edge.

'Change of plan, sure enough,' said Wilson quietly from the far end of the boardwalk. 'One you hadn't figured on. This is your restin' place, Scoone. A graveyard.'

Scoone swallowed as he turned, his gaze fixed on the marshal's levelled Winchester, his mind throbbing with the odds of twin Colts blazing vital seconds ahead of a steady rifle's roar. 'Sonofabitch,' he hissed.

Wilson's face was dark, impassive, the scar white and lifeless. 'Been a long time, Edrow,' he said. 'Three years since the shootin' at Long Rocks. Remember?'

Scoone muttered words that crawled from his mouth as no more than sounds. His eyes shifted left, right, to every dark cranny where, like a trapped insect, he might scurry. But not without biting.

He began to sweat. No chance of Quire being of any use while he remained here on the boardwalk. He needed to draw Wilson to the street, in open space where Halfneck could shoot from an upstairs window. It had worked before. Many times.

'You shot a young fella in the back at Long Rocks,' said Wilson in the same contained tone. 'Remember him? He was just turned seventeen. Right there along of me that mornin'. Stood at my side.'

Scoone's fingers twitched. This was going nowhere. Who the hell was Wilson talking about? Damn it, he had shot men in a dozen back-of-nowhere towns. Young, old, who cared? His fingers twitched again. Maybe Halfneck had realized the situation. Maybe he was on his way, moving quietly down the stairs, through the saloon. . . .

Wilson's rifle shifted the merest fraction.

'To hell with you, Wilson!' Scoone exploded like something put to the torch, reaching for his Colts in one flashing move.

It took four deliberately aimed, precisely targeted shots to down Edrow Scoone, the last of them blazed from close range to spin him like a whipped top from the boardwalk to the street.

He had growled and cursed, threatened and condemned with every gasped breath of his last seconds. The twin Colts had cleared leather, only for one of them to thud uselessly to the boards. The other had roared ahead of Scoone's cackled laughter as he watched the shot raise fresh blood from the marshal's wound, but the Winchester's third blaze had buried itself deep in the gunslinger's chest, and the fourth settled it.

Wilson caught his breath, winced and slid his fingers through the blood oozing from the bandaged wound. He moved to the batwings, pushed them open and stepped into the still shadowy gloom of the bar.

'Easy with that piece, Marshal. On the floor if you please.'

Halfneck Quire was halfway down the stairs from the first floor rooms, a Colt in the grip of his good hand, the bound bulk of the other held across his chest. His lips were parted in a sneer that slid to a grimace with sudden stabs of pain; his eyes were glazed, bloodshot with booze, but his legs and balance were steady.

He prodded the Colt forward, flicked his glance quickly to where Lanky hovered over the still sprawled body of Drone, and grinned. 'Only one thing for it, ain't there, Marshal? All down to me. Me and my gun. And you just standin' there, your piece at your feet. All that effort of killin' my fine friends wasted. All for nothin', 'cus now you're goin' to die anyway, and I'm goin' to be the one left standin', free to ride where I want, when I want . . . to tell the story as how Marshal Wilson never did settle the full score with Edrow Scoone and his partners, 'cus when it came down to it, there was Halfneck Quire facin' him at the last, a Colt all set to blaze. Ain't that just somethin', eh?'

The roar and blaze when it came was from somewhere higher; somewhere in the darkness of the gloomy level fronting the rooms. It bit through the saloon as if to devour, rushed at the walls like a tornado released from a trap, and echoed high and thin until it seemed it would pierce the ear of every living man in Random on that day.

And when at last it faded across the morning and died, Patsy Newbutt stood at the head of the stairs, stared at the dead body of Quire face down on the floor, handed a still smoking Colt to Doc Marchman, and smiled.


'She shot him in the back. Never hesitated. But, hell, it still took some nerve.' Lanky Joe poured a line of drinks ranged along the bar and invited the town men to help themselves.

'She was steady as rock,' said Pop Ryder.

'Fittin' justice it should be Miss Patsy who fired the last shot,' murmured Charlie Mint.

The men nodded their agreement.

'Where'd she get the gun, that's what I want to know?' asked a man in a chewed straw hat and stained dungarees.

'That was my doin',' said Doc Marchman, making his way down the stairs. 'Took it on myself to arm as many of the girls as I could, includin' Patsy. Glad I did, too.'

'You bet,' smiled Ben McKellan. 'Why, if there'd been

nobody up there with a piece when that scumbag Quire had Wilson at his mercy . . . Hell, could've been a whole sight different story.'

'We've been one helluva lot lucky,' said Pop Ryder. 'There's been deaths, sure there has. Good men gave their lives, but they didn't die for nothin', not while ever these old bones of mine can find the strength to move and help rebuild this town and put it on the map where it rightfully belongs.'

'Here, here!' chorused the town men.

'We'll rebuild, Pop, every last plank, make no mistake,' chimed a man, raising his half empty glass. 'Here's to Random. Long may it live!'

The gathering toasted the town and its future.

'But what about Wilson,' said Cuts Bailey, finishing his measure. 'Rode out faster than I can blink. Why'd he do that after all he'd done, and him with that wound bleedin' like it was. Hell, you'd have figured on him gettin' Doc to fix it.' Cuts grunted to himself. 'What do you reckon, Sheriff?' he asked, turning to where Caulk watched the street from the batwings.

Caulk waited a moment before turning to the men. 'I'll tell you somethin' about that marshal I didn't know 'til Doc told me.' He paused, scanned the street again, then continued, 'Some of you were watchin' best you could from wherever you could when Wilson finally faced Scoone out there on the boardwalk. If you were, you'll have heard the marshal speak of a young man shot at his side during Scoone's raid at a place called Long Rocks. That young fella – just turned seventeen – was Wilson's son.'

A deep, chilled silence filled the bar.

'Says a whole lot about Wilson, don't it?' murmured

Pop. 'Man was on a mission, about as personal as it gets.'

'And I'll tell you somethin' else about the man,' added Doc. 'You're all of you wonderin' why he rode out like he did, with, as you saw, a bleedin' wound. I'd done what I could for him here in the bar before he slipped away out the back durin' the fire. And I let him go. Never raised a finger against him.'

'Why was that, Doc?' asked Charlie.

Doc's gaze moved slowly over the faces watching him. 'Because the fellow was dyin'. Doctors back East had confirmed an incurable disease that left the man with only months, mebbe as little as weeks, to live. I figured it while I was treatin' him. He admitted it to me, told me about his son, and said as how time was fast runnin' out for what he had to do and vowed he would do before he died. I reckoned I had no choice but to let him go.'

'Nor did you,' said Ben McKellan. 'Any one of us would have done the same.'

The men talked quietly among themselves before lapsing into a thoughtful silence again.

It was Lanky Joe who cleared the darkening atmosphere. 'Hey, now, let's be grateful, eh?' he grinned, opening a new bottle to pour a fresh round of drinks. 'I reckon on a toast – to Marshal Wilson who's given us the future. Marshal Wilson!'

And when the toast had been drunk and the saloon settled to the familiar hum of a day's usual business, with the girls and Patsy Newbutt emerging from the shadows in their best dresses, and Sheriff Caulk, Doc Marchman and a dozen town men drawing up plans for the reconstruction of Random, Lanky Joe collected his besom and stepped out to the boardwalk.

There was work to be done.